SMOKE
OVER
GOLAN

Harper & Row, Publishers

New York, Hagerstown, San Francisco, London

THE JEWISH PUBLICATION SOCIETY OF AMERICA
• PHILADELPHIA

SMOKE OVER GOLAN

by Uriel Ofek

Translated by Israel I. Taslitt

Illustrated by Lloyd Bloom

Smoke Over Golan: A novel of the 1973 Yom Kippur War in Israel
First published in Hebrew in 1974 under the title *Âshan Kise et ha-Golan* by
M. Mizrachi, Publishers, Tel Aviv.
Text copyright © 1974 by Uriel Ofek
Illustrations copyright © 1979 by Lloyd Bloom
Translation copyright © 1979 by Harper & Row, Publishers, Inc.

FIRST AMERICAN EDITION

*This edition was published for the members
of the Jewish Publication Society of America
(by arrangement with Harper & Row, Publishers, Inc.).*

Library of Congress Cataloging in Publication Data
Ofek, Uriel.
  Smoke over Golan.

  Translation of Âshan kise et ha-Golan.
  SUMMARY: A 10-year-old Israeli boy's adventure near
the front during the Yom Kippur War between Israel and
Egypt and Syria.
  [1. Israel-Arab War, 1973—Fiction] I. Bloom,
Lloyd. II. Title.
PZ7.O326Sm 1979   [Fic]   78-22488
ISBN 0-06-024613-8
ISBN 0-06-024614-6 lib. bdg.

Contents

To Neot-Golan

Everything has come and gone now. Everything—the evacuation, the shelling, the fire. The fear. Everything must begin anew. We shall do it—and soon no one will know what happened here. Our farm will be as it was before the war: The irises will bloom beneath the window, the chickens will cluck in the henhouse and wake me from my sleep. Dad will go out on the farm again (he's a real cowboy, my Dad is), and Mom will receive guests and treat them to cakes. I'll be going out to the grove to see if the apricots have ripened. Then in the evening we'll all sit in the room, opposite the TV set, and watch "A Look at the News" or "Guardians of the Forest." Maybe, by the time this story sees print, a new series will be shown, one I'll

1

really like. I've learned that life is full of surprises.

I'm quite sure that soon no one visiting us will see any signs of what happened here in the twelve days between Yom Kippur and Simhat-Torah. Almost nothing: maybe the ruins of an abandoned army post, a small gouge in the big boulder, or maybe an empty shell casing in the gully, across from the post. That's all, just about. Well, there's also the small scar on my arm. I've almost forgotten about it.

Since soon nothing will be left here to tell about those days, which seem like a nightmare, I've decided to sit down and write about it all, to tell the story—just to make sure that it is remembered. As the days go by we shall begin forgetting them, little by little. Memory grows faint, new things crowd out the old. That's when you can open the book and read and recall what really happened.

It did happen, all of it.

I shall begin at the beginning, maybe even a bit before that. It's important.

We've been living here at Neot-Golan for six years. Before that we lived in Hadera, but I don't remember much from those days. They seem to have happened even before I was born (who can imagine it?). Well, I was only about five and a half at the time.

But one particular evening I remember very well.

The two of us—Mom and I—were sitting in the room. Mom was in the armchair, knitting a sweater. I was on the floor, with my drawing pad. The radio was on. Suddenly I heard Dad's pickup truck stopping by the window. Its door slammed shut, the house door opened, and Dad came in—tall, tanned, hair blown wild, his bright eyes on us.

"Everything's in order," he said, shedding his coat. "We're going up tomorrow."

That's my dad—doesn't talk much, and always to the point. Says just what has to be said, but he does a lot, without end, and anything you want. Even if he's my dad, I must praise him a bit. First, he deserves it—all the way. Also, it's true, just as everything I'm telling here is true.

To make it short, after Dad was discharged from the regular army (he was a major in the Armored Corps), he went back to live in Hadera. For a while he drove a truck, carrying flowers or chicks. But he found it awfully hard—after the Six-Day War—to go back to normal life. *Now* I understand him very well; I too find

3

it hard to get back to normal life. But let's go back to my dad: After he was discharged from the regular army, his work didn't satisfy him. He wanted to do something special—settle in a new spot, be busy with something unusual, exciting. And so he kept traveling from one place to the next, all the way down to the Sinai border, back up to the north, traveling and looking around— talking to people, until he came up with something worth the trouble.

"Everything's in order," he announced, as he came into the room. His voice was a bit tired but very excited. "Tomorrow we are going up."

"To the Heights?" Mom asked.

"Affirmative," Dad replied, in his favorite army talk. "You'll have everything ready?"

"Yes. Everything. Now go and wash up. The water is hot, and so is supper."

I was very young then. I understood more or less what my folks were talking about, but how could I have known that this talk meant that our lives were going to change—and so suddenly!

Two days later—it was on Wednesday, actually—we climbed into the truck. Dad was at the wheel, Mom next to him, and I sat behind them in our wicker chair, among the furniture and the crates. The next minute we were off on our long trip, to a new life about which I knew nothing.

We drove northward, through Wadi Ara and past Afula, and still kept going north. We passed Tiberias and Rosh-Pinna, and here the truck turned to the east. We crossed the Jordan River by Bnot Yaacov Bridge, past the old British customs depot, and kept climbing. For about half an hour the truck continued along the narrow road. I had a look at the route on both sides; the road was lined with gray basalt. Deep and narrow gullies. Small stone huts scattered here and there. A few cows grazing among the bushes, under the watchful eye of an Arab shepherd. Once in a while an abandoned concrete post would flash by. A military vehicle passed us, and the driver waved to me.

Suddenly the truck turned onto a dirt road and kept bumping and grinding through large and empty fields. I was afraid I couldn't hold out, but suddenly Dad cut the motor and the truck stopped.

"You can climb down, Eitan," he said. "We're home."

I jumped down from the truck and stood next to my dad. I saw an old but pretty stone house, in the shade of oak trees. A bit beyond it, close to each other, were two other buildings: a barn with a dozen cows in it and

5

a stable with horses. Another building, the chicken coop, was still being built. All around us were light-brown hillocks, and to the northeast the snowy crest of Mount Hermon glistened in the distance.

"We're home," Dad repeated, and I could hear the tone of pride in his voice.

"Neot-Golan," said Mom. So that was the name of our farm! Mom was smiling, but I thought I heard a hidden sigh.

Everything was so new, strange, mysterious, and inviting, but I was tired from the long trip and wanted to go inside the house and rest. I turned toward the porch, but before I had taken three steps, a loud and frightening bark suddenly came from behind me. It wasn't really a terribly threatening bark, but I was terrified. After all, I was only five and a half; and I was scared even more when I saw the dog—big as a horse—coming at us from the direction of the barn.

"Mommy!" I cried out in terror. I was sure the dog was going to tear me apart.

"Down, Nicky." I heard a commanding voice. The dog immediately sat down and pricked up his ears, suddenly friendly.

A man came out of the stable. To me he looked like a giant: very tall, his hair falling down to his shoulders, and a rough black beard covering his face. He was wearing creased khaki shirt and pants, and a large revolver swung in a holster at his hip.

"That's a good fellow, Nicky," he said to the dog, patting his head. Then he approached us, slapped Dad on the back cheerfully, and said to all of us, "Welcome, all!"

"What's doing, Albert?" Dad asked him.

"No problems," Albert replied in his deep voice. "Well, how about going inside? I've got food ready for you. For me, too."

"Let's go in, then," Dad agreed. "But first, say hello to each other. Eitan, this is Albert. Albert, this is Eitan."

That was how we first met each other, and that was the beginning of our long friendship. I must have smiled at him, because he looked me over with his friendly eyes and said, "A right good fellow. You ready to go out with me to the pasture?"

I nodded silently; I must have been too tired to say anything. But I did understand: Albert was Dad's friend, and he was with us because he was working on the farm.

We went into the house. Mom went to the kitchen and Dad opened the windows.

I climbed up on the first chair I saw, curled

up—and that's the end of what I remember of our first day here, in Neot-Golan, except, perhaps, the loud barking from between the barn and the stable.

A Teacher in Army Uniform

The first months at Neot-Golan flew by swiftly. One day came hard on the heels of the other. I don't know how, but already I felt at home, as if I had been born here and hadn't been anywhere else in my life. The years in Hadera faded away.

I've just tried to sit and go over what happened during the first year, but it's no use. Everything is mixed up, and I can't tell what came before and what came after. It's as if someone had picked up a bunch of photographs and mixed them up, like a large tossed salad. . . .

Here I am with Albert, on the porch. Nicky is at his side. Albert turns to the dog and addresses him softly: "See here, Nicky. This is Eitan, and he's a good fellow. So come on now and be good friends. Good?" Then he turns to

me and says: "See here, Eitan. This is Nicky, and
he's a marvelous dog. A bit frightening, but he
wouldn't hurt a fly. Well, a fly maybe, but not
you. He's yours, too, you know, so let's all be
friends." Then, seeing that I was too scared to
make a move, he went on, "What's there to be
afraid of? Look at me!" With this, he thrust his
hand into the dog's giant mouth, right past his
sharp teeth, then took his hand out. "You see?
Nothing to be afraid of." But that in itself was
enough to frighten me.

Two or three days later, Nicky and I were the
best of friends.

I remember something else:

10

Dad and I are sitting under a large oak in the pasture. Opposite us the cows are grazing peacefully. A warm sun sparkles above the high mountains of the Golan Heights. Nicky is darting back and forth among the cows, keeping them together. Dad is checking his revolver. Now comes Albert, riding his horse, Roxy, and says, "My stomach tells me it's time for lunch. What does your stomach say?"

And here's another scene:

I'm standing next to Mom in the hatchery, looking at the long row of eggs lying side by side, and I see a wonderful thing: An eggshell cracks, breaks open, and out comes a tiny

11

chick, covered with wet yellow down. Another egg opens, another chick comes out, a whole family of chicks comes to life. I stand there, mouth open, and Mom looks at me and says, "Aren't they cute? Now we have to feed them."

One more scene:

I'm standing on a low rock, alone. All around, the hillocks are still gray in the dawn. I look out to the east and see the sunrise and a newborn day. But this is something I can't put into words. It must be seen—and felt.

One day follows another, and one scene comes after another. The order in which they come isn't really important. But there was one evening worth telling about in detail.

That evening my parents were at the dining-room table, as usual. Dad was going through the newspaper and Mom was sewing a button onto his shirt. I was sitting on the floor, working on my Erector set. Suddenly I felt Mom's eyes on me. "Do you realize how old he is?" Mom asked Dad, nodding her head toward me.

Dad also glanced in my direction. "About six and something."

"He will be six and a half next month," Mom went on. "What are we going to do?"

"About what?"

"The child must have some schooling."

"Who says he's not learning?" asked Dad, as he laid the paper aside. "On the farm you learn something all the time. You know that."

"I mean school learning."

"You mean books and such," Dad said. "That's fine. He's got plenty of time before he goes to college."

"This is no joking matter, Danny," said Mom, putting the needle away. "First of all, there's a compulsory school attendance law in this country. You know that. But what's more important— don't you want our son to be able to read?"

"He already reads the cows and the dog like a book—right, son?" Dad laughed, then became serious. "Sure, Eitan's got to learn many more things, not only how to read. What do you think about being his first teacher?"

"Me?" Mom stared at him.

"Yes, you—Tirza Avivi in person. Why not? You went to the Teachers' Academy, didn't you?"

"I did—but only for a year." Mom smiled sadly. "Then the war came and I volunteered for army duty. Then you came and married me. Now you really wouldn't want a teacher who isn't qualified to teach your son, would you?"

"No—but what do you suggest, that we send him to a school in a nearby kibbutz?"

"No, no. But—"

"Or are you proposing that we open a special Eitan Avivi school, here at Neot-Golan?"

"And why not?" Mom demanded seriously.

Being the subject of the discussion, I should have listened more. But I can't remember anything else—maybe I fell asleep just then. Anyway, I don't know what my parents decided that evening.

The next day I went out to the field with Dad and Albert, as usual. I wasn't of much help to them, of course, but, as Dad said, that was my learning period. Today I know that it was a happy and helpful period that taught me a whole lot, and I wish all kids could have it. I learned how to keep my eyes open, to listen for voices and sounds, to get along on little. To toughen myself. These were things which would do me a lot of good later—nature study, farming, friends, sports and exercise, love of country, fieldwork and GADNA, the young people's national service, all woven together.

Anyway, that evening, after supper, Mom said to me: "Eitan, tomorrow you're not going out to the field."

"Why not?" I asked. "Are we going on a trip somewhere?"

"No trip. You're going to school."

"Really?" I asked, surprised. "Which one?"

Before Mom could answer, Dad broke in. "You've already managed to arrange it?" he said in surprise.

"Well, you see I did."

"How did you do it?"

"Very simply. Neot-Golan is an independent settlement located in a development area. As such, according to the law, it has a right to a school of its own. I put through some telephone calls, made some contacts, explained and argued a bit—and it's all arranged."

"So fast?"

"There are some problems," Mom replied airily, "but we shall have a school."

"A special school for Eitan," mused Dad. "Hard to believe."

"That means that tomorrow my teacher will be here?" I asked.

"That's what they promised me," Mom said. "Tomorrow you begin going to school, Eitan, and that calls for a little party."

I wanted to ask more—who and what—but I decided to wait and find out for myself. I was already forming the habit of not asking about

15

things I could find out for myself. That's the way to do it. Also, Mom had promised a party.

Anyway, the next day Dad and Albert went out to the field, and I remained in the house. Mom and I went to the southern room, which was once used as a toolshed. It had an entrance all its own. She took out all the tools and the trash, cleaned the room, hung a curtain across the window, brought in a table and two chairs, and said, "Well, Eitan. This is going to be your classroom. How do you like it?"

"It's swell!" I said.

Mom sat down at the table, put a large chunk of cardboard she had cut out from an apricot carton on it, and wrote something with a crayon, in large printed letters. I looked at the pretty letters curiously, then asked (since I didn't know how to read), "What does that say, Mom?"

"Just a minute," Mom said as she went on writing. "I'll be finished soon."

When she was done, she looked it over, drew her fingers across the letters, and read out loud for me:

STATE SCHOOL, NEOT-GOLAN

"And now," she said, "let's go and hang the sign up in its place." She took a few thumbtacks, and together we tacked the sign to the door, on the outside, right in the middle.

"Where's the teacher?" I asked, looking around.

"I hope she'll come soon," Mom said. "Wait for her here. I'm going to feed the chickens."

I stood on the porch and looked out toward the winding dirt road. It was quiet. Nothing moved there, and the landscape looked like a photograph without a frame. After a few minutes of fruitless waiting, I went down to the yard and on to the flower bed near the gate. I never like to spend time doing nothing. I pulled up the weeds and from time to time gave a look out to the dirt road.

Suddenly I saw a column of dust rising from the road to the sky. Out of this dust came an army jeep. It drew near the gate and stopped. A girl soldier hopped out and waved good-bye to the driver. The jeep backed up, raising another cloud of dust. The girl came through the gate, her leather handbag hanging on one shoulder. On her head was a pert army cap. She came forward slowly, looked at the scenery all around, at the farm building, then stopped near me.

"Excuse me," she said. "This *is* Neot-Golan?"

"Affirmative," I said, talking like my dad, as I threw away a crabgrass root.

"Fine," said the girl. "My name's Ricky. I'd like to talk to— But wait! You're Eitan, aren't you?"

"That's right," I said. "How did you know?"

"Simple. I'm your teacher. They told me at the base: 'You're to go there to teach Eitan Avivi.' And so, here I am!"

Her answer really mixed me up. "A teacher— a soldier?" I wondered.

"Exactly. Or, as you say, affirmative." She smiled. "A teacher—a soldier. You may not know it—but then, how could you? There are many of us soldiers and teachers. I enlisted in the army as soon as I graduated Teachers' College, and they sent me to teach, near the border. And so here I am, at Neot-Golan. And now, Eitan, after this long introduction, how about taking me to the classroom?"

I liked my teacher right away. Ricky was pretty, with smiling eyes, light-brown hair clipped short, cute dimples in her cheeks. I felt it would be fun to study with such a teacher.

We approached the classroom and stopped at the door. Ricky read the sign aloud: "State School, Neot-Golan," and nodded in approval. We went inside, and I had the feeling that another world was about to open up for me.

"Come, let us sit at the table," said Ricky. I sat down next to her. From her briefcase she took a notebook, two pencils, and two books. "We shall have to order a blackboard," she said, looking around the room, "and a classroom record book, but we can still start without them. Now, Eitan, what's the first thing you would like to learn?"

"How to write my name," I said promptly. "I already know what the first letter is."

"Fine! So we shall learn how to write your name. Here, look at the sheet. I am now spelling: E—I—T—A—N. Now you try it."

And that is how my first day in the classroom began. I liked it.

The Tiniest School in the World

The days kept flying by swiftly, as if they had wings. Perhaps it was the strong wind blowing up here on the Heights that pushed them along. The morning hours were set aside for study. Every morning I sat with Ricky in the classroom. She taught patiently, quietly smiling whenever I made some silly mistake. I have no idea how I did it, but suddenly I found myself reading and doing problems in arithmetic. Once I even found a mistake Albert had made in his measurements when he laid out the new chicken coop.

I must admit I really enjoyed my lessons. It was lots of fun, to sit with Ricky and listen to her explaining how to put words together, showing me how to add and subtract. We talked about the new people coming into the land, about truths and lies; we learned new songs, or strolled out in the fields and learned the names of the birds and flowers. To this day I can't understand how a teacher can work in a classroom of thirty or forty pupils. The way I was learning seemed so natural to me that I don't think I would have agreed to sit in a large class and watch Ricky teaching other children. How could that be? She was *my* teacher, wasn't she?

In the meantime, the room was beginning to look more and more like a real classroom. We put up a calendar on the north wall, and on the others we hung up a map of the country, a picture of the President, and all kinds of posters and slogans. Now it felt like sitting in a real classroom.

During the week Ricky stayed with us and slept on the farm. On Fridays she went out to the dirt road and hitched a ride—usually in the same jeep—to her folks' home in Nahariya. On Sundays she was back again for another week of school.

One Friday, after Ricky had been with us for almost two years, as we were sitting in the classroom and talking about the coming national elections, the door opened and a soldier in uniform stood at the entrance. A sergeant. I guessed that he was the driver of the jeep—and I was right.

"Ricky," he said, "I have to leave earlier. Can you make it?"

Ricky glanced at her watch. "Fine, Nimrod. Give me another minute and we'll be on our way." She turned to me. "We'll get back to our chat on Sunday, O.K.?" With this, she went around the room, quickly putting things in order.

The sergeant peered at me, then burst into laughter. "I'll be a monkey's uncle!" he said merrily. "One teacher—one pupil! This is the tiniest school in the world! It's not to be believed! I've got to tell this to my brother-in-law!"

Ricky put on her hat. The two said good-bye to me and went out to the jeep, at the gate.

A few days later—I don't recall how many, but that's not the point—I went out with Ricky for a lesson about nature. We stopped by a loquat tree in bloom, and Ricky pointed out what made up the blossom: the stigma, the stamen, the petal, and the receptacle. I took a flower and slowly pulled it apart, unaware that a white Simca had driven into the yard and someone was getting out of it.

"Beg pardon, may I snap some pictures?" the

22

newcomer asked, coming nearer. Before we could say a word, he went on, "Thanks ever so much! But do go on with your lesson. Just pretend I'm not here."

The new arrival, we learned, was Nimrod's brother-in-law, the newspaper reporter Yigael Shapira. He was a stocky fellow, but he moved around quickly enough. His hair was swirly at the forehead, and a thin moustache lined his grinning lips. He spent the whole day with us and made himself very much at home. He sat with us in the classroom and went about with us outside, asking questions and jotting the answers in his black-bound book. Then he snapped pictures, played with Nicky when the dog wandered into the classroom, and even stayed for lunch. He did break in on one lesson, but Ricky was very polite. After all, he *was* Sergeant Nimrod's brother-in-law!

In the afternoon, seeming very pleased with his visit, Yigael bade us a cheerful *Shalom*, got into his Simca, and took off.

"Quite a nervy fellow," said Ricky, watching the car disappear in the distance, "but he does make a good impression. And now, Eitan, back to class."

"Why?" I wondered. "We don't have school in the afternoon."

24

"We won't do any studying," Ricky assured me. "You will do your homework, and I shall get ready for tomorrow."

That's Ricky for you, doing her own homework for tomorrow, as if she didn't already have the stuff down pat.

About two weeks later, in the afternoon, the red van of the postmobile pulled up at the farm gate (it usually came every other day with a piece of mail or two). The driver reached out through the window and handed me a rolled-up magazine. "It's for you," said the postman, and drove off. Sure enough, my name was there. This was the first time I had ever gotten anything in the mail in my name.

It was a new issue of *The Children's World*. I unrolled it, took one look at the front page, and gave out with a yell. "Hey! Ricky, Mom! Come quickly! Look at this!"

"This" was a front-page picture of Ricky and me standing in the doorway of the classroom, with half a sign showing. We flipped the pages until we came upon a story with a double headline:

Eitan of Neot-Golan: The Only

Pupil in the World's Tiniest School

The three of us sat down and began reading the article. It had six pictures: Ricky and I in the classroom and in the yard, Nicky and I, and others. I felt kind of queer, looking at myself and seeing my name in print (for the first time I also saw my face in profile). Ricky was right: Yigael Shapira knew his stuff. He took whatever he had seen and heard here—nothing special, to my way of thinking—and turned it into an interesting story. Sure, here and there he went overboard, but Ricky said that's how reporters are. Since the story was well written, I will copy it here. That way I won't have to write about it:

Teacher Ricky [*began the article*] puts a problem in arithmetic on the board: 54 − 28. She doesn't have to ask who's ready to solve it. Eitan Avivi, an eight-year-old with golden hair, gets up from his seat, goes to the board, and writes the answer. It's correct. This exercise, and whatever the teacher does in the classroom, is for him alone. That's because Eitan is the only pupil in the class—the second grade. In fact, he's the only pupil in the whole school!

Surprised, are you? Small wonder. I too was surprised when I first heard about it.

The school is on the Neot-Golan farm, opposite the mountains of Bashan on the Syrian heights, about a mile from the border. Eitan, the only youngster on the farm, went there almost two years ago, and he seems to be quite happy in this out-of-the-way spot.

"At first," he told me, "we lived in Hadera, where I went to Esther's kindergarten. But my father didn't like it there. Things didn't interest him enough, and so we came here. . . . I like it very much," Eitan said, "and I'm not bored at all." [*Here Yigael Shapira went on to describe the farm.*]

Now I said that Eitan is the only member of the class, but that's not quite so. If the classroom door is open, Nicky sneaks in and sits down opposite the table, just like a regular pupil. Nicky is Eitan's dog, and he's big enough to be in the second grade.

Every morning, at eight on the dot, Teacher Ricky waits for Eitan at the classroom door. Eitan has to walk no more than a dozen yards to get there. There's no bell, of course. At nine there's a ten-minute recess, plus a longer one for a snack, from ten to ten-thirty. The work then continues until twelve noon.

Ricky, now serving in the regular army, had this to say: "Teaching one youngster is, I think, much harder than teaching a whole class. At times it gets boring for the teacher, or for the pupil, although he may not be aware of it. It is not always easy to work up to a long chat. Of course, Eitan cannot discuss things with other youngsters. But, like the others, he must do his homework and keep his books in good order."

27

"What about punishment?" I asked.

"He doesn't have anyone with whom he can raise a rumpus, so I really don't have occasion to punish him. Last month he did very well in arithmetic and Hebrew. Our program of studies comes from the Ministry of Education, and I also teach him Bible, geography, drawing, and singing. I want to say," she added softly, "that Eitan is really part of my life, much more than ordinary pupils are to their teachers. I am also very close to him. It's quite natural."

To Eitan, this way of learning is also quite natural. He knows no other. He loves his lessons, and enjoys the trips in the area. In the afternoon he works with his father, doing farm chores. He is there when the cows come in from the pasture, helps his mother in the chicken coop, waters the garden. Briefly, a full and interesting day.

The last question I asked Eitan was what he wanted to be when he grew up. He looked at me with his big blue eyes and replied, straight to the point, "What do you mean, what? I'll get in the saddle and ride out with the cows to pasture, just like my dad."

Yigael had put together quite a story. I decided to keep the magazine, and I still look at it once in a while.

I didn't think grown-ups read this children's magazine, but it seems they do. After the story appeared, other reporters came to talk with me. Their reports, in the morning and afternoon papers, were much shorter, but most of them appeared inside fancy borders. Dad said that this was meant to give it "appeal." When I asked him what "appeal" meant, he said, "It's set up in a way to make you want to read it. If a woman gives birth to five children, or if a man bites a dog—that's a news item with 'appeal.' You want to know more about it."

Even the TV people came around and put me in front of their cameras. Honest! Taking the pictures and recording the whole thing took hours, but when at last they showed me on the TV set, I was on for no more than two minutes.

All these visits began to annoy me. Ricky did say, "You see, Eitan? Now you are famous, and thanks to you I am also famous." But this being famous was no great shakes. Sure, at first it was a lot of fun seeing my picture in newspapers or on TV, but in time it became boring. Mom had to keep preparing refreshments for the uninvited guests. Quite often she had to get up and excuse herself. "I beg your pardon," she would say, "but I have chicks waiting for me to take care of them."

All of us were happy when all this fuss finally died down. Albert said, "Now that the big bash is over, maybe now we'll be able to get in some work."

As I think back, I recall several reporters asking me the same question: "Tell the truth, Eitan. Don't you feel lonely in this faraway place?"

"Lonely?" I asked back. "Why should I feel lonely? My mom and dad are here, and so's my grown-up friend Albert, and our dog Nicky, and the horses. I'm just not lonely."

"What we mean," said a woman reporter, "is friends your age. Don't you ever feel that you'd like to play with other youngsters, get into a bit of mischief, you know?"

"I don't like mischief," I told her, "and who says I don't have friends to play with? It's just that I don't have much time for play."

But that night, when I was already in bed, I thought it would be real nice if I had a friend my age.

Before many weeks passed, I found one.

My Friend Saleem

My ninth birthday passed with nothing special to mark it. The Seder night came and went, and we were in the middle of the Passover holiday. Ricky had gone to Nahariya, so the school was closed, and I was enjoying ten days of vacation.

Every morning I went with Albert out to the pasture. The cows ambled along peacefully as Nicky pranced around them, barking. Dad remained behind on the farm to finish building the shelter. The rising sun was turning from red to gold.

"How do you like that!" said Albert. "Only a week ago it rained cats and dogs here, and now—just take a look! The sky's blue, the field's green, everything's cheerful, and the cows'll have a good time."

"You said it," I agreed. Indeed, the skies were

31

blue, with no more than a spot of cloud here and there. The field was dotted with yellow chrysanthemums amidst the green. We guided the herd toward Sugar Valley and settled the cows down in the shade of an oak tree. We had given the valley this name because on the slope of the hill beyond it was the Syrian village Sukri. The village was on the far side of the border, inside Syrian territory. I could see the village clearly, the day being so bright. There was nothing—not a fence, nor even a line along the ground—to show the border. If I wanted to, I could get to the village inside an hour, stroll about its small houses, and be with people whom I could now see only from far away.

"It sure is a beautiful day," I said.

"Salamtak," replied Albert in Arabic, keeping an eye on the cows. He always liked to throw in a few words of Arabic.

"You really think spring's here to stay?" I asked.

"Inshallah." He nodded sagely. "Allah is great."

I knew that Albert's folks had come from North Africa, and all of them spoke Arabic. But Albert insisted that all Israelis should be familiar with the language, especially those who, like us, lived close to the border.

"You should ask your teacher Ricky to teach you Arabic, *ya haboob*," he once urged me. "If she can't, I'll do it—and someday you'll thank me for it." At the time, Albert didn't know how close he was to the truth. Anyway, thanks to Albert's prodding and to TV (the Beirut TV station), I had begun adding more and more words in Arabic to those I already knew, but I didn't have many chances to use them, and it didn't look as if I ever would.

The sun kept climbing higher in the sky. The only sound that broke the silence was an occasional bark, contributed by Nicky—at the cows, at a lone jackal streaking across the field, or at the stalks swaying in the wind. Albert was whittling away at a stick with his long-bladed pocket-knife. I looked at Roxy, tethered to the tree trunk, and at our ten cows, spread out in the field. For no reason at all I began counting them, by name: Afura, Huma, Rimona, Stavit. Something was wrong. "Hey, Albert!" I said. "Do you see Galila?"

"Galila," returned Albert, whittling away, "is in the barn."

"Why?"

"She'll be giving birth today," he said calmly, then jumped up as if stung. He snapped the blade shut. "*Hamor* that I am, a real jackass!" he exclaimed. "Galila is giving birth and I'm sitting here! Maybe she needs help. I should be there to see that everything's going alright. *Yah-rabeti!*" He kicked at a clump of earth and glanced at me out of the corner of his eye, as if urging me to come up with an idea. I had one: "Why don't you take a hop home, see what's doing, and then come back? What do you think?"

"Not a bad idea," replied Albert, then looked at me sharply. "You won't be scared here, all by yourself?"

"Scared!" I cried. "Why, all of a sudden? Don't forget I'm nine years and two weeks old. Besides, I'm not alone. Nicky's here with me."

Albert gave me a fond look and clapped me on the shoulder. "You're a real *shatr*, a fine fellow," he said. "O.K., I'll head for home and bring back the lunch." Untying Roxy, he mounted the horse, then turned to Nicky with a farewell wave of his hand, which the dog returned with a brisk bark. Albert gave a tug to get Roxy going, and off he galloped to the west. I was alone with the dog and the cows.

Well, it was kind of a new feeling, being left all by myself, without Dad or Albert around. I wasn't scared—why should I have been? There was nothing to be afraid of, but still my heart began to beat faster. I felt excited, and as I think back, it might have been that I felt the responsibility. It wasn't so simple—to be alone with the herd, for the first time. Deep inside I knew that I was too young for this kind of duty, and I was hoping that it would be over soon, without any surprises.

I took a look about me, at the cows, Sugar Valley, the Sukri village, Mount Hermon in the distance, the army post. I looked at the trail leading to the farm—as if I might already see Albert coming back. I wanted him to return, with lunch and with his open grin. But nothing was moving along the trail. Overhead a hawk was soaring high.

Suddenly Nicky turned toward the valley and began barking loudly.

"Keep quiet, Nicky," I called to him. "There's nobody out there!" The echo of my voice resounding in the valley made me feel safer. I wanted to believe that there was no one out there.

Nicky kept barking angrily, as if to drive off some unwelcome visitor. I looked at him and thought, *Maybe there is someone out there, among the rocks. A man or an animal?* I felt my fear giving way to curiosity. Who could it be? I headed for the slope and began picking my way among the rocks—slowly, carefully, more curious—and a bit more scared. I followed a path across the slope, bending low among the rocks. Nicky was following me, much to my relief. With that hound around, nothing was going to happen to me.

I was about halfway up the slope when I heard a thin voice calling from below, "Sussu! Ya Sussu!"

I came around the bend of a big rock, and I saw him: a short boy, barefoot, about my age, dressed in a long shirt and worn pants. An Arab boy, with a dark face and unruly hair. He stood there, craning his neck, as if looking for something. No reason for me to be scared—that I knew.

"Hi!" I called out to him.

He hadn't seen me, and my voice caught him by surprise. He stepped back a bit, and kept his eyes on me as I came slowly toward him. For a few seconds both of us made no move—just looked at each other. At last I said: *"Shalom!"* in Hebrew.

"Salaam!" he returned in Arabic, in a husky voice.

Nicky wagged his tail, once, and barked.

"Quiet, Nicky," I said, and Nicky fell quiet. I turned to the boy. *"Ismi* Eitan," I gave him my name, in Arabic. "*Shu ismak.* What's yours?"

His eyes lit up. "Saleem." Then his face darkened again. "Sussu, ya Sussu!" he kept repeating.

"What are you looking for, Saleem?" I asked in Arabic (I may not have said it right). I swiveled my hand at the wrist, back and forth—the Arab way of asking a question. He said, *"Jahash."* The word sounded harsh, but it told me what he was looking for—a young donkey. Just then I felt grateful to Albert for having taught me some Arabic; I would have liked to know more. I decided to help my dark-skinned friend, who must have crossed the border in his search for his lost donkey.

I turned to Nicky. "Now listen, you hound," I said. "Saleem's little donkey has gone astray. He must be somewhere around here. Let's go find him. What do you say, scout?"

Of course I didn't expect Nicky to understand what I was saying, but it's a fact: He pricked up his ears, gave a businesslike bark, took a look at me, at Saleem, all around, and headed back toward the rocks. I followed him, with Saleem a few paces behind. Nicky moved past the rocks, but no donkey. I stopped, letting Nicky go on alone, and turned to Saleem to tell him that I too was sorry. Just then Nicky gave a loud bark,

37

up ahead. I saw him bounding toward a small narrow gully which cut across the slope; it was hidden by the undergrowth. I rushed to the spot, Saleem at my heels. Nicky had stopped at the edge of the gully and was barking into it. *"Taal hon,"* I said, telling Saleem to come near. He was still wary of Nicky's bark.

We peered down into the gully. There it was: a small gray donkey, a bag of bones—that's how thin he was—with large, moist eyes. He was jammed tight in the narrow gully, and couldn't budge. He raised his head, looked at us sadly, and wiggled his long ears.

"Sussu!" Saleem cried out happily. He slid down into the gully, threw his arms around Sussu's neck, and lovingly caressed his back. The donkey's skin trembled at the boy's touch. How had Sussu gotten there? He must have lost his way, or something may have scared him and made him lose his footing. Once down in the gully, he didn't have enough strength to pull himself out. He just stood there and waited for help.

Well, we got him out. It took a lot of work. We pushed and pulled, puffing hard and sweating. Nicky kept advising us, with his bark. At long last, Sussu was out of the gully.

A voice came to us from up above. "Eitan!

Eitan!" Albert had come back from the farm—and I was nowhere around.

"Here I am!" I yelled, and Nicky joined in, even more loudly. *"Taal,"* I said to Saleem. "Let's go." We reached the rocky slope just as Albert came up.

"What've you been up to?" he asked.

"Here, say hello to Saleem," I said, instead of answering his question.

Albert's eyes didn't leave my face. "Where have you been?" he demanded sternly.

"Saleem's donkey got lost," I explained. "Nicky and I went to help him find it. We did, in the gully. That's Sussu."

Seeing that I was alright and that the cows were grazing peacefully, Albert calmed down, and the grin came back to his grizzly face. He looked at Saleem, standing there, abashed, and asked him a few questions in his throaty Arabic. Saleem told him the whole story—that he lived in Sukri with his parents, brothers and sisters, that his little donkey had gone astray; had it not been for me, he might have never found him. He was very thankful, and hoped that, with Allah's help, we would meet again.

Saleem jumped on Sussu's back, almost flattening the poor animal. Again he thanked us, waved his hand, and headed east, his bare feet almost scraping the ground.

"*Haboob*," said Albert. "He's a good kid."

"What's new on the farm?" I asked. "Has Galila given birth?"

"She did. We have a new calf in the family." Albert headed for the tree. "Come sit down, and we'll have a bite. I'm good and hungry, and you must be starved, after using up your strength to get the poor donkey out."

As usual, Albert was right. We sat down and did away with the lunch.

"I hope we'll meet again." That's what Saleem had said—and we did, almost always at the same spot, the field at the end of Sugar Valley. Most times he came riding on Sussu. Our friendship grew from week to week, and even though he lived in Syria and had to cross the border to get to me, nobody stopped us from meeting—not guards, not an army, not the United Nations peace-keeping force. My parents and Albert wanted us to meet, which was to be expected.

We didn't play much, because our games were different. Also, our talk came in snatches; he knew only a few words of Hebrew, and my Arabic was still far from good. But we didn't need many words, for our kind of friendship; it's

41

hard to explain, but you get the idea. At times Saleem played with Nicky, throwing his stick far away and having Nicky dash and retrieve it. He also liked to pat the cows on the neck, but most of all he loved Albert's fine horse, Roxy. Once, when Albert was in a very good mood, he even let Saleem mount the horse.

That's how we spent the time. One day, in late summer, just before the High Holidays, we were in the field. The sun was dipping toward the mountains of Galilee, coating the houses in Sukri with gold. It was time for Saleem to leave. He took a small reed pipe out from under his shirt and handed it to me.

"Take it," he said. "A present from me to you."

"You're giving it to me?" I asked, staring at it.

"Yes," he said. "It's for you."

"*Shukran*, thanks," I mumbled. Now I felt that I should give him a gift. I reached into my pocket. My fingers closed about a hard object— and I felt better. "Here, this is for you," I said happily, handing him my new penknife (it had three blades, a bottle opener, and a corkscrew). "My present to you."

Saleem was overcome. "*Shukran, shukran,*" he repeated.

"*Shalom*, Saleem," I said.

"*Lehitraot,*" he replied in Hebrew.

We parted and went back to our homes.

The penknife . . . I wonder if my friend Saleem still has it.

Lookout Post

I sat in the classroom, writing a story. Ricky sat across the table from me, checking my answers on the arithmetic test. Then she noted something down in her diary. Ricky should have already received her discharge papers from the army, but she had decided to sign up for another term of regular service, which meant that she would be teaching me for another year or two. Also, Mom had asked her to stay on, and Mom has a way of getting people to go along with her. Ricky knew how I felt about it, and I knew her reason, too; she had a boyfriend in the nearby army camp. Anyway, Ricky stayed on, and I was very happy.

I raised my head, looked out at the Bashan mountain ridges outlined against the blue sky, and went on writing:

44

"My best friend's name is Saleem. My other friends are Albert, my teacher Ricky, and Nicky the dog. [I first wrote "my teacher Nicky, and Ricky the dog," but I corrected the silly mistake right away.] But Saleem is the only friend of my own age, so I think he's my real friend.

"Saleem is an Arab boy—a Syrian, really. He lives in Sukri Village, across the border, and several times a week he crosses over and we meet in the field, talk and play. Talking is a bit hard because of the languages, but we get around it one way or another. Yesterday I brought my soccer ball along, and we practiced kicking goals. At first Saleem's kicking was funny, off to one side or too high, but once I gave him a few pointers he got the idea, and both of us were happy.

"I hope that my soldier teacher won't tell her commander that Saleem has been crossing the border. After all, he's my friend and we like each other."

A horn honked twice outside, followed by a loud whistling of the first notes of "A-Marching We Will Go." I looked up. Ricky was already heading for the door.

"What's up, Nimrod?" she asked.

"Important matters," the sergeant-driver answered. "You ready?"

"In a minute. Come on in. Eitan, are you done with your story?"

"Almost. But I want to go over it again. O.K.?"

"O.K. plus," said Ricky. "That is important." She added a note in her diary and put it away. I went over my story and put the date down at the bottom. Nimrod, leaning against the door, looked at his watch. "The party will be starting in half an hour."

"What party?" asked my teacher.

"Come on, Ricky. Don't make like you don't know."

"I really don't," claimed Ricky. "Be a good fellow and remind me."

"We're dedicating the new wing in our post, remember?"

"Oh, sure," said Ricky, a bit annoyed with herself. "I'm ready."

I also remembered. For several weeks large trucks had come rolling past our farm on the way to the post atop the lookout ridge, north of us. Dad and Albert had talked about some "big project going on there," but to me the whole fuss didn't seem important. Sure, I knew the post was there and that Nimrod was serving there, with the other soldiers. But even though the post was near enough, it seemed far away—

out of my range of interest. Certainly it never entered my head that I would have a chance to visit it.

But here, all of a sudden—a party! And my teacher Ricky had been invited to be there.

"Can I come along?" I blurted out.

"What did you say?" asked Nimrod, staring at me.

"I said can I come along," I repeated. "I've never been to the post, see? Now I've got a chance . . ."

Ricky and Nimrod looked at each other. She nodded her head, for him to agree. Nimrod muttered something about a "military secret," that it didn't depend on him, to which Ricky said, "On my responsibility." Finally Nimrod gave up. "O.K. Come along. It seems you've got pull with certain people."

At that moment I liked Ricky even more, and that's how I got my first look at the post, which was to play an important part in this story.

I handed Ricky my composition notebook, and we said good-bye to Mom, and climbed aboard the jeep. A short ride along the dirt road, a turn to the east—and there we were on the narrow blacktop road. I sat in the back and whistled, trying hard not to show how excited I was. I was glad that Nimrod and Ricky hardly paid any attention to me. The jeep moved right along, hurdling the bumps in the road. Seven or eight minutes later it came to a halt.

I jumped down, to find myself between two camouflage nets. They blended in with the colors of the countryside so well that I hardly noticed them. Under the nets crouched two giant tanks. This was the first time I had stood so close to a tank. What can I tell you? From nearby it's real scary.

"Come on," Nimrod said, and the three of us went near the entrance to the post. At first all I saw was a mass of concrete built in among the boulders and surrounded by barbed wire, the kind we call accordion. Near the entrance we came upon a tall, thin soldier with a red moustache, dressed in paratrooper boots, with an Uzi gun hanging from his left shoulder.

"*Ahlan*, welcome, come on in," he said. Then, looking at me, he asked, "Who's this?"

"I'm Eitan," I said.

"Glad to meet you. I'm Asher. Have you got a movement pass?"

"No," I replied. "What's a movement pass?"

"It's a regulation. What about an entry pass, or some other document?"

"I don't have any, but Ricky . . ."

"Sorry." The sentry barred my way. "This

48

here's a very secret place. Without a proper pass, even the Chief-of-Staff can't get in."

I was sure he was serious, and I looked pleadingly at Ricky, but she stood off to one side and didn't say a word.

"The army's the army," said Nimrod. "We don't play around."

I was in a tight spot. For a moment I thought that somehow they had gotten to know about Saleem. I stood there, abashed, trying hard not to break into tears. Finally Ricky took pity on me and came to my rescue; "Come on, Asher'ke! Stop throwing your weight around," she said to the sentry.

Asher grinned and let me go in. That very day we became good friends.

The party was very gay—or, as Albert says, *ala keifak.* We sat in the mess hut around tables filled with cookies, chocolates, soft drinks, and all kinds of good things. An army song-and-dance unit played the latest hits and led us in community singing, with each soldier trying to off-key all the others. Then Ricky led a quiz on the country's geography (she let me join in it, too). The post commander, Captain Zerubavel, had some words to say:

"We have the honor and privilege of garrisoning the forwardmost post on the Golan

49

Heights. Two hundred yards away from us is no-man's land, and beyond that the Syrians are set up in full force. Zahal, our defense army, is depending on us to live up to its reputation. Each one of us knows exactly what his duties are. Should the enemy try to cross the border at this sensitive point, he will find us ready for action. We shall throw him back and carry the fighting into his territory. O.K., that's all for the speech, now hear this: We've got to get this party swinging!"

Well, it sure did swing, and how! I was there about an hour and a half, and I enjoyed every minute of it. After the party, Nimrod took Ricky and me for a tour of the bunker; to me it looked like a strange underground fort. I visited the soldiers' quarters, a kind of long and narrow bunkroom, like aboard a submarine—rows of bunks above each other. The soldiers were at rest—"grabbing quiet," as Nimrod put it. Two were playing dominoes. Another was reading *The Case of the Flashy Burglar.* Asher'ke was sewing a button onto his shirt. In the corner bunk a soldier with curly hair lay staring at the picture of a pinup girl on the opposite wall.

"Hey there, young man," Nimrod said to me when he saw what I was looking at. "That's for adults only."

I went to have a look at the command room. It was filled with wires and light bulbs, large maps and telephones, cardboard files and buzzing communication instruments. When I had seen all there was to see, Captain Zerubavel shook hands with me and said, "That's it, fella. It was nice having you here. But remember— not a word about anything you saw here, not to anyone, is that clear?"

"Sure," I said, and that's why I'm not saying any more about what I saw and did in the bunker.

I said good-bye to everyone and went back home in the jeep with Ricky and Nimrod. We got to the farm worn out but pleased, as they say.

That was the beginning. Later, over the next months, came more visits—on both sides. My parents decided to "adopt" the post (I agreed heartily), and after that the soldiers started dropping in, even without an invitation—for a shower, laundry, phoning home. They peeped into the classroom and tried to annoy Ricky.

Nimrod and Asher'ke came most often. Nimrod would go straight to the classroom to say hello to Ricky. Asher'ke, the redhead from Bitzaron the settlement, went to the barn, to see the cows and do "milking exercises," as he called it.

"I want you to know," he said to me, "that working in the barn is what I like best. When you come to my home, I'll show you what a real modern cow barn looks like, with all the gadgets. And our cows—each one is a beauty queen."

I also liked to visit the soldiers on the post, especially on the Sabbath. They all knew me. Nobody asked me for a pass. In good weather I used to walk to the post—forty minutes of fast walking on the road. Once I tried to see how long it would take me to get there if I cut across the field, but Nimrod quickly warned me: "Don't you dare, you hear? This field is mined."

That's all I needed.

I loved to see how the soldiers were taking care of the tanks, cleaning their weapons, wrestling. One time they had a speaker talk to them for about an hour and a quarter about the economic problems of the state. I tried to listen, but understood almost nothing.

I also loved talking with the soldiers, when they had the time. Most of all I talked with Asher'ke, who almost always seemed to have time for me. Maybe it was because he wanted to make up for the rough welcome he had given me the first time we met. Maybe, but I'm not sure. He asked me things, told me about his friends in his village, his family, and what-not.

"You know why I like spending time with you, Eitan?" he once asked me.

"Why?"

"Because you remind me of Ami, my younger brother."

"So!" I said. "And if I didn't remind you of your brother, you wouldn't want to?"

"No, of course I would," Asher'ke hastily tried to correct himself. "You're some kid! But because the two of you look alike, I feel that you're a member of my family, see? I haven't seen him for a thousand weeks."

He went up to the peephole in the eastern wall of the bunker, picked up the field glasses, raised them to his eyes, and slowly scanned the rocky plain below us.

"So!" he muttered. "They're keeping on the move, down there."

"Who?" I asked.

"The Syrian tanks."

"Can I have a look?"

He gave me the large field glasses, and after a few tries and turning the thumb wheel I could also see them. More than a mile away from us, three or four yellow tanks were moving from north to south among the rocks and bushes, their cannon muzzles pointing upward.

"I don't much like the looks of this," said Asher'ke after I returned the field glasses.

"Why?" I asked. "Do you think they'll dare start up with us?"

"Who knows? Zerubavel says there's no such danger. According to the Chief-of-Staff—he told us—we'll be having years of quiet here. But who knows? Life's full of surprises, *ya haboob.* Lots and lots of them!"

He replaced the field glasses in their leather case and sat down on an empty crate. For a while he sat still, looking at the firing slit. Now he was a different Asher'ke, no longer thinking about the barn or his younger brother, but about something else altogether. Suddenly he took a strange-looking black pistol with a long barrel down from the shelf.

"What kind of a pistol is that?" I asked, curious.

"It's a rocket gun," he explained. "In a time of danger, you can fire a red streak up toward the sky. That's a call for immediate help." His voice was quiet and his eyes taut. "Your farm,

Eitan, Neot-Golan, is the closest point to our bunker. You know what? I think that we ought to set up some kind of direct communication between us."

"What kind of communication?" I asked.

"Something simple but one that works," he replied. "A field telephone or a walkie-talkie, so that if anything unusual happens here, or if you need help from us, we'll be able to get in touch with each other."

"But Asher'ke," I said, "everybody, even the Chief-of-Staff, says that we will have years of quiet here!"

"Life is full of surprises," said Asher. "Lots and lots of them!"

This Asher'ke, once he got an idea into his head, didn't rest until he got it done. Before the month was over, there was a connection between us and the post. It was a simple signaling device: The minute either of us wanted to make contact, all we'd have to do was to press a button; as soon as there was a buzzing sound, the contact would be made. On a Sabbath evening Asher'ke put the device on the shelf in my room. "Now, Eitan, we'll make one try to see if the thing works. After that, we'll use it only in case of real emergencies. You'll remember?"

"Sure I'll remember," I said. But all around everything was so quiet and peaceful that by the next day I'd forgotten all about it.

Yom Kippur

A new year dawned, on the world and on Neot-Golan, a year of many hopes, even a year of peace. Amen!

But on the morning after Rosh Hashana things began looking different, as if small clouds were beginning to gather from beyond the ridge—winter clouds to which we paid no attention.

On the first day, I sat in the classroom, answering the greeting cards which had arrived late. I replied to Yigael Shapira, the reporter, to a girl in Dimona—her name was Simcha—who had read the piece about me in the paper and wanted us to be pen pals—and to Aunt Sophie in Canada. Maybe one or two others; I really don't remember.

The next day my mother went to her parents in Hadera. She was in the last months of her pregnancy, and as she felt a kind of weariness, she decided to spend the few days until she gave birth in the city, where she would be near a hospital. After breakfast she packed a small valise and boarded the little truck. Dad sat down next to her.

"Take care of the house, Eitan," she said, putting her hand on my shoulder. "I'll try to be back home real soon." For a moment she was quiet, then said, "Until now I thought I'd be glad for a change of scenery, but I'm already beginning to feel homesick."

"Everything will be just fine, Mom," I said to her. "The main thing is that you come back all well, with my little sister, the way you want it."

"If it's a boy we won't chase him away," Albert joined in. "As my old man says, 'One son is a sign for more sons.'"

Dad started the motor, took Mom to Hadera, and returned alone, with four bags of cement.

The week passed quickly. The first clouds of autumn sailed across the sky. With them flew the storks, on their way south, resting at times on the tall squills. At night I heard the wind whistling between the chicken coop and the barn, and a loose shutter banging somewhere.

On Thursday Ricky left for her Yom Kippur and Succot vacation.

58

"Have a nice holiday, Eitan," she said. "I may be back with a new teacher, to take my place."

"But you will come to visit me, if you can, won't you?"

She nodded, smiling, and went to the gate.

On the next day, Friday, Albert and I took the cows out to Sugar Valley. Dad stayed on the farm to do Mom's work—in the coop, the garden and the kitchen. I rode the colt Jordan and was in a good mood. Around my neck hung the strap of the field glasses—Asher'ke's gift to me for the new year.

"Today I'll be meeting Saleem," I said. "He promised to be here by noon. I'll show him how to look through these glasses."

"If he promised to come, he'll come," said Albert.

But Saleem didn't come.

I waited for him—an hour, two, three; still no sign of him. I stood near the tree and trained the field glasses on Sukri. Maybe I could catch sight of him in the distance. Nothing. I saw an empty road, deserted houses. Not a soul in sight. The air was filled with a strange uneasy quiet, a kind of emptiness, finally broken by Albert. "Come on, fella, stop standing like a pole. Have some grapes."

"Thanks," I said, accepting the cluster. "But why didn't Saleem come today?"

"*Allah baaref*, Allah knows," Albert replied. "Why, why? When he comes tomorrow you'll ask him."

I popped three grapes into my mouth and again scanned the large plain, north and south of Sukri. Suddenly I called out in surprise, "Hey, Albert, look over there!"

He looked—and there sure was something to see. Across the entire field we saw humps and mounds, set row by row, of one size. I recognized them immediately: They were camouflage

nets, with something hidden under them. I knew very well what this "something" was. Straining my eyes, I could also see people moving among them, but I couldn't tell what they were doing.

"Do you see what I see, Albert?"

"Sure do," he replied grimly.

"Those are tanks," I added.

"I know, I know. Tanks. So what? As long as they're under the nets, you don't have to worry."

"But you've got to understand," I tried to explain.

"And even if they're not under the nets, there's nothing to worry about. Want more grapes?"

Nicky jumped up and grabbed a grape from my hand. Suddenly a thought crossed my mind. Perhaps there was some connection between the camouflage nets and the fact that Saleem hadn't come today. But the thought came and went, like a flash, like the storks flying above us, or like the two butterflies chasing each other among the field flowers. By now the sun was high; everything was warm and pleasant, and whatever worry I had quickly disappeared.

We returned to the farm in the afternoon, going back early because of the holiday. When I entered the house I found Dad talking to Mom on the telephone.

"Everything's fine, Tirza," he was saying. "Today I gathered thirty-two eggs. One got broken. I prepared a meal fit for a king, as you wrote in the note you left on the table. Well, the fellows are returning from pasture. Love and kisses, partner. Regards to the folks—and take care of yourself!"

After we got cleaned up and dressed we sat around the table for our evening talk. Dad said that after Succot, work would begin on an asphalt road to the farm. Albert said this would be a good time to repair the little bridge at the turn of the road. Suddenly I said, "You know what, Dad? Today in the field we saw some Syrian tanks on the other side of the border, under camouflage nets. There were at least ten of them, if not more."

"Many more," said Dad, and I thought I heard a slight sigh in his voice. "Our lookouts have been reporting that they are thickening their lines along the border."

"Also, Saleem had promised to come today and he didn't. Do you think there's a connection?"

"Between Saleem and the tanks? No, I don't think so. They're just getting ready for their fall maneuvers. Nothing to worry about, young man. Let's get onto something else."

The talk turned to the elections, which didn't interest me very much.

The night was very quiet, or maybe it seemed that way because of the nights that followed. Anyway, I slept soundly, without waking even once, until, in the morning, Nicky's loud barking came into the room, along with the sound of a car stopping at the gate, a honk of a horn and, a moment later, a knock on the door.

I jumped out of bed and quickly opened the door. I saw a stocky fellow in military uniform, without stripes.

"Good morning," he said. "Your Dad home?"

"Sure he's home," I heard Dad's voice behind me. "What's the idea of waking people up so early, especially on Yom Kippur?"

"So I'm to blame because they declare an alert on Yom Kippur?" the newcomer said. "Here you are," he said, handing Dad a printed page.

"An alert?" repeated Dad. "Why, all of a sudden?"

"How do I know? It's an order. You and Albert are to join your unit as fast as you can. Your wife and boy are to go down to Ginosar."

Dad gave the visitor a wondering look; I had never seen him so confused.

"You mean to tell me that there's an order for me to vacate Neot-Golan? Well, see here. I didn't come here to be evacuated . . ."

"It's not only Neot-Golan. All the settlements along the border are being cleared."

"It doesn't make sense," Dad said, but he began dressing.

"It does, it doesn't. That's an order," said the messenger. I could see he was getting more impatient by the minute. "Main thing is—are you ready?"

Albert, standing off to one side, suddenly remarked, "His wife isn't here, so if we go to our unit, who'll take care of the boy?"

"That's smart thinking," said the other man. "For your information, a bus will be here by noon to pick him up. Let's get going."

"We're coming," said Dad. "Give us just five more minutes." He looked out through the open door. "But I don't get it. Who'll look after the farm? Who'll take care of the livestock?"

"They'll have to shift for themselves," said the messenger. "But why make up problems? You'll be back in a day or two. Take my word for it."

Five minutes later Dad and Albert were ready to leave. I went with them to the truck. Dad halted, looked around, and said to me, "All right, son. Until noon you'll be the only man on the farm. You won't be scared, being alone?"

"Why should I be scared?" I said, trying not to be. "It's my home, isn't it?" I had a hard time thinking straight.

"And until they come to pick you up," added Albert, "spread out the feed for the cows and the chickens, and don't be stingy. Let them have enough for tomorrow."

"Everything will be in order," I assured him.

"And lock all the doors before you leave," said Dad, from the driver's seat.

"O.K.," I yelled. "Come back soon. You hear?"

"Sure thing, commander, sir." Dad grinned and started the motor.

I was alone on the farm. I looked at the open gate, the farmhouse, and I got a funny feeling. This was the first time I'd been here alone—no Dad, no Mom, no Ricky, no Albert. They were called up—they got up, and left. Alert, what kind of alert? Soon the bus would come to pick me up, and that would leave no one to watch the farm, except Nicky. But what had happened? Maybe it had something to do with the tanks under the camouflage nets? Or maybe it was a big maneuver or something like that?

The big dog started bounding around me impatiently.

"You're right, Nicky," I said. "Why think about it too much? Instead of thinking, let's get on with the work. There's plenty of it, and the time's short."

There sure was enough work. Even on Yom Kippur, the livestock had to be fed. I took fodder to the barn and the stable, scattered feed for the chickens in the coop. I even milked the cows,

66

with the help of the milking machine. All that worked up an appetite. I went into the kitchen, fixed a bite for me and Nicky, and washed and dried the dishes. I felt good: Mom would've been proud of me!

I watered the garden, then turned on the transistor! Not a sound. No wonder, it was Yom Kippur and no broadcasting is done on that day. I sat down on the porch and tried reading *Treasure Island,* but after I read the same line three times, I closed the book. It was noon, and the bus would be arriving any minute.

I went from door to door and tried the keys. Each one worked fine. Then I took the field glasses and went past the gate and out of the yard, and clambered to the top of a nearby boulder to look around. What a deep silence! The large flag was waving easily above the lookout post. The camouflage nets were hiding the dozens of tanks under them. On the slope of the hill, the houses of Sukri were dozing in the sun.

I was bored. Maybe I should leave a note on the door—"I am at the lookout post"—and go visit the soldiers in the bunker? Say, that was an idea. I wouldn't feel so lonely. But my orders were to wait for the bus. I began longing for my friends. For Saleem. Saleem—maybe he was waiting for me right now, at the tree!

Again I lifted the field glasses to my eyes and looked eastward, to the valley. I couldn't believe what I saw. I blinked several times; was I dreaming? Even as I was looking, and as if by a magic wand, the camouflage nets were being peeled off, all at one time, and drawn back like brownish-yellow waves, and the tanks beneath them stood clear. At that moment, a tremendous blast deafened my ears, and a cloud of dust rose and covered the lookout post.

"It's War, Fella"

"It has begun!" These were the first words that crossed my mind. But there was no time for more. I stood there, for how long I don't know, as if turned to stone. Only my knees shook, and my eyes moved back and forth across the war that was catching fire all around me.

A column of tanks began rolling across the plain, cannon pointing at the lookout post, probably at other targets, too. The middle cannon seemed to be pointing straight at me.

A shell whined as it streaked across the sky high above me—first far away, then shrieking closer, forcing me to duck, then disappearing to the west, where it landed with muffled thunder and a strange silence.

The shells fell on top of the post and around it, in a series of booms, covering the ridge with dust and smoke. Overhead jets came streaking—a quartet of MIGs cutting across the sky with terrifying speed, toward Mount Hermon.

The thunderous noise around me kept getting stronger. I had never imagined such noise. I felt like a small pebble being ground up by giant wheels. As if the earth was trembling beneath me and would split, and I'd fall into a black pit.

I stood there on the boulder, without moving, scared out of my wits. I was afraid that if I were to move my foot, I'd fall and not be able to get up. Then I bent down a bit and waited for the awful noise to stop or at least lessen a bit. It couldn't go on forever. This was probably nothing more than a "burst of fire," as we called it. The Syrians had started it—and we'd silence them. Then one of our cannon in the post fired toward the tanks approaching the border. A white mushroom came out of the turret of one tank; that tank stopped, but the others kept coming, and the noise didn't lessen. If anything, it grew worse as more shells kept falling. One of them landed where the dirt and asphalt roads met. Another shell streaked above me like a kite, then a third . . . and a fourth . . . and a tenth. Nicky, at the foot of the boulder, was barking and crying at the same time.

"We've got to get into the house, Nicky," I shouted. "No, not the house. The shelter. Come on!" I yanked my foot away from the boulder and set off at a run to the gate. Inside the coop, the chickens were in an uproar. The horses were stamping about. I rushed down the steps of the shelter and threw myself down on the folding cot, huffing and puffing, almost choking with coughs. Still, I was thankful that the soldiers from the post couldn't see me. And Ricky—what would she think of her scared pupil! Now, as I think of it, that's how anyone would have behaved. I sat there, gasping for breath, glad that the shelter was keeping the terror away from me.

I had hardly been down in the shelter before. I didn't like it. It was dark and gloomy, and I'd always hurried to get out again into the bright sunshine. Now I was thankful for it. I lit the lamp on the shelf. Nicky sat on the bottom step, ears and nose poking out. He was protecting me, and was I glad to have him around!

I sat on the cot, without moving, and listened to the thunder of the explosions outside. It seemed to come from another world. I felt small and miserable. Who would have believed it— they had all gone away and left me here alone, in the midst of this awful noise. Maybe a miracle

would happen, and someone would suddenly appear and say, Come, we're getting out of here. The bus! Maybe it was on the way to pick me up and take me to Ginosar? But how could it travel, out there among the shells? Maybe it had started to come, but on the way, suddenly, an enemy shell had come down and . . . No, no, I mustn't think of such things!

I sat there and tried hard to think about nothing—just sit and look at my good big Nicky. But how could I *not* think, for the roll of cannon thunder kept coming into the shelter? Two shells fell—one far away, the other so close that it shook the wall I was leaning against. A moment of quiet, then two more bursts, one after another, and my heart echoed their whines. My poor heart was about to burst like the shells!

Another burst of thunder. I shut my eyes tight—perhaps that would cut down the noise. But the blasts kept coming, without a stop. And yet at the same time I felt my fear growing less and less. It didn't go away altogether, but it wasn't as strong. Once you got used to the sound, it wasn't so terrible.

Now I was beginning to understand what was happening. The concrete walls and sandbags were guarding me. They reminded me of the lookout post bunkers. I looked around. On the shelf, next to the matches and candles, was a first-aid kit, with bandages, tape, and all kinds of medicines. Two army blankets were spread on the cot, and two canteens hung from nails in the wall. I checked them; they were full. That was just like Dad; he had everything down to the last detail. Maybe he had felt that someday they would come in handy.

I sat down again on the cot. What else was I to do? I don't even know how long I sat there, not moving, not knowing what time it was. Time seemed to freeze, to be motionless. The explosions outside sounded like the irregular ticking of some giant clock.

Tick! In the midst of a blast the electricity in the shelter went out. I guessed that a shell had hit the electric pole or had snapped the wires. I didn't light a candle but sat there in the dark. Once my eyes got used to it, I shifted myself toward the steps. Now everything looked gray. Suddenly I saw Nicky moving away from the steps, down to the floor of the shelter, growling. I could see the reason; a stream of water was flowing down the steps.

What now? I must have been so scared that I hadn't shut the faucet tight. Couldn't be. I remembered that I had shut it. Water's an expensive item up here, and even at a time like this—especially at a time like this—every drop is precious.

"Come on, Nicky! Let's get out of here," I said to the dog.

We went up the stairs and I pushed the door open. As soon as we were outside my eyes closed to keep out the bright sunshine. When I finally opened them and looked around, everything had changed. The smoky air was acrid with gunpowder. The upper section of the stable roof had been sheared right off, as if with one sweep of a giant knife. The horses were still milling around, but I didn't dare go inside. The distant electric light pole, near the dirt road, was standing on a slant, and two of the wires were torn. Our pretty yard was under water.

So that was it: A shell had hit the water line (I couldn't tell where) and the water was flowing into the yard. What was I to do? I'd have to run to the gate, turn off the main valve by the water meter, before the pond grew into a sea, or before the shelter filled with water.

At the first break in the shelling (or maybe I was used to it by then), I sloshed through the huge puddle, with Nicky at my side, until I got to the valve. I tried to turn the handle, but it wouldn't budge. I tried it to the left and to the right, with the same results. It hadn't been turned for some time, and the threading must have gotten stuck. Still, I couldn't let the house and everything in it be flooded. I grabbed hold with both hands, turned and turned, until the stubborn handle gave way slowly, and a few seconds later the flood was over.

"That's it, Nicky!" I said, straightening up. "Back to the shelter."

We made our way back, again through the puddle. Before going down, I took another quick look around. How near had their tanks managed to come? I looked out at the plain, golden in the setting sun, and not a tank was in sight. Had we thrown them back, or had they changed direction? I heard explosions from over the main road, and I had the answer: They were taking the easy road to the Heights. Anyway, the farm was off to one side, and they weren't likely to come near it. What luck!

I leaned against the wall and wiped my hands on my shirt. Suddenly the sky above me was shattered by a loud noise, and two planes came into view, streaking northwest. Only two? Behind them came two others, trying to get on the tails of the first two. This was an air chase, two Syrian MIGs pursued by two Israeli Mirages, and it lasted no more than two minutes. Before I could see clearly what was what, the first MIG turned into a ball of white smoke. In a twinkling it began flipping over, lost altitude and, its tail hidden by black smoke, dropped at an angle and crashed on the ridge to the north. A column of smoke mushroomed upward, followed by a muffled explosion. It was a frightening sight. I knew that it was an enemy plane, but I was not happy; why, I don't know. But I suddenly felt older, as if a year had passed since yesterday. So here I was a grown-up, with no idea of what I should do.

"Well, what do you think?" I turned to Nicky. "O.K. Let's go in—but into the shelter or the house? All right, let's go into the kitchen and see what we can put together for supper."

We went in. I made a sandwich of yellow cheese, took out a tomato. I gave up the idea of scrambled eggs and went to make tea, but when I turned on the faucet, not a drop of water came out—naturally, since I had turned off the main valve outside. I had to be content with a glass of milk from the cooler, with two spoonfuls of sugar.

Nicky and I began eating. I turned on the transistor: The radio must be broadcasting, in this situation. I was right. A familiar voice came over the air. It was the Prime Minister. Golda Meir spoke very slowly, and I brought the tran-

77

sistor close to my ear, so as not to miss a word:

"Today, at about two o'clock in the afternoon, the forces of Egypt and Syria launched an attack on Israel. They carried out a series of assaults by air, armor and artillery in Sinai and on the Golan Heights. Our defense army is prepared to repel the attack. All of us are being asked to be ready for every burden and sacrifice to defend our existence. We must be worthy of our sons, who are now carrying out their duty with courage and valor, at their posts and in the settlements, on the firing lines of all the fronts."

Well, Eitan—you've heard it. This is no local clash. It's war, and you, young fellow, are suddenly alone at the front, right in it. As I was listening to the radio, I felt that the Prime Minister had me in mind also, when she said "our sons who are doing their duty in the posts and settlements." If I only knew what my duty was, right now! Who was there to tell me what I should do? And suppose they did get to the farm? They'd find a boy of ten and a half. No, I wouldn't let them find me. I'd find a place to hide in. Perhaps the shelter, or in the hayloft in the barn, or maybe on the roof. I knew every nook and cranny on the farm, and I could get around quickly. If I hid nobody would find me, except Nicky, perhaps.

The shells kept bursting, near the road. If I had had a weapon I'd have felt much safer. Maybe Dad had left his revolver at home? I had once seen it in his desk drawer. I opened the drawer—there was nothing inside. I moved away, and as I was passing the door to my room, I heard a loud buzzing sound coming from the shelf. I peered into the dark room. What was it?

A second later I had the answer. It was Asher'ke's communications instrument. The buzz meant I should go to the post.

Wounded in the Bunker

"We'll use it only in real emergencies,"
Asher'ke had said, when he brought the instrument. And now someone was using it, trying to
get through to me. There was no doubt about
it: They were calling me to come to the post. I,
Eitan, had to go help the soldiers. And when
you have to go, you forget about being scared.

I went out to the porch. Night had fallen.
Nicky followed me.

"Now you stay home, Nicky," I told him.
"Wait for me right here, O.K.? Watch the house
until I come back. Even if I don't get back soon,
you wait for me, Nicky."

He understood, that clever Nicky of mine.

I went down to the yard, toward the gate.
Near the walk I found an old cane I must have
put there a long time ago. I picked it up and

went out to the dirt road. The cane made me feel safer.

I walked fast. The rocky plain was under cover of darkness, but a round moon shone overhead, as on every Yom Kippur night. The long narrow road was also lit here and there. All kinds of vehicles were stuck, most of them still afire, like burning torches.

I came to the crossroad and turned east. I walked fast but not on the road. Something told me to walk along the shoulders. I walked without pausing or looking into the burnt-out trucks or disabled tanks.

As I was feeling good about the fact that the road was empty, I saw what I took to be three armored troop carriers coming toward me. "Must be Syrians," I said to myself. I was plenty scared. Of course, I was only a boy, much too young to be in the army, but they must not see me, or else . . . I looked about quickly. A little ways ahead was a culvert, under which drainage water passed during the season. Without thinking twice, I threw myself down beneath it and lay on my stomach without moving. The roar of the motors was now much nearer, and a moment later the trucks rumbled overhead. The soldiers aboard were yelling above the noise, but I couldn't catch a single word.

The trucks disappeared and again there was silence all around. From somewhere in the distance came a muffled blast, followed by a burst of gunfire.

I crawled out from under the culvert. The night wind cut across my skin, and I felt cold. All I had on was a shirt.

I walked even faster, still holding on to the cane, until I reached the yard of the post. How the place had changed over Yom Kippur! The barbed-wire fence was down. The yard was empty. The tanks weren't there; they had withdrawn or had been sent to some other place. A scorched, overturned command car was at the fence. The sharp smell of smoke mixed with dust lay heavy in the air. I ran up to the bunker. Its outside walls were pitted with shell hits. The place was as silent as a cemetery.

I hurried down the steps into the bunker, then advanced slowly. The only sound I could hear was my heart beating.

"Hi, there!" I called out. "Anybody here?"

At first there wasn't a sound to break the deathly stillness. Then I heard a voice from the communications room: "Eitan? Is that you, Eitan?"

"It's me," I answered. My throat had suddenly gone dry. "Where are you, Asher'ke?"

"Here—by . . . by the transmitter."

I headed for the communications room, feeling my way in the darkness, until I found him. He was lying on his side, by the table, knees bent under him. His arm reached out until it felt me. "It's good that you came, Eitan," he said hoarsely, trying to stifle a groan.

"What happened to you?" I asked, though I had a good idea.

"Here, on the table, you'll find a flashlight. Put it on."

I pressed the button. A faint shaft of light lit the room and came to rest on my friend, the wounded soldier.

"I got in the way of a shell fragment, with my shoulder . . . out there in the yard. . . . Later I crawled here and called you. . . . I thought . . ."

"But how do you feel now?" I broke in.

"Kind of weak, and it hurts. Think you can bind the wound?"

I took his first-aid bandage out of his pocket. I helped him prop himself up against an empty crate, and he told me how to treat him. First I tore away the wrapping, drew the bandage tight, and looped it again and again. Then I moved his arm back under the shirt.

The smell of the blood made me a bit dizzy.

"Thanks a lot, Eitan," he said, with a slight groan. "It sure is good to see you here."

"What now, Asher'ke?" I was ready to do anything for him.

"The canteen . . . I'm awfully thirsty."

I unscrewed the canteen and brought it to his lips. He took big gulps, as the water trickled down on his neck and chest.

"That's a heck of a lot better," he said, propping himself up more comfortably.

The flashlight was casting a big shadow of me on the wall. "Are you here alone, Asher'ke?" I

remembered to ask.

"The others got orders to move out. They took the tanks to the post at the intersection. I covered them, until I got hit. . . . Just couldn't make it to the tank. And Amiram," he said, and suddenly fell silent.

"Where's Amiram?" I asked.

Asher'ke nodded toward a corner. I saw a stretcher, on which lay a figure entirely covered with a blanket.

"Is he asleep?" I asked, although I knew better.

"Forever," said Asher'ke.

I was shaken. This was the first time I had stood so close to a corpse; and this was someone I knew. Good that he was covered and I didn't have to see his face. But I remembered Amiram very well; he was the blond curly-haired fellow from Netanya, the one who liked to lie in his bunk and look at the pinup models on the wall, with a playful grin on his lips. Now Amiram's eyes could see nothing and a blanket was covering his face.

"Eitan!" Asher'ke's voice broke into my thoughts.

"Yes," I said, returning to his side.

"What's doing at the farm?"

"I was left there alone," I replied.

"And they didn't get to you?"

"No. I think they're pretty far away from the farm."

"That's what I thought," he said. "You're off to one side." He paused, then went on. "Do you think you can help me, Eitan?"

"How?"

"To get to your place, to the farm. I think both of us would be safer there." A slight grin came to his lips. "What's more, I'll be close to the cows. That'll make me feel closer to home like nothing else."

86

"Let's go," I said. I also wanted to be on the farm, just then.

"O.K. Give me a minute, and we'll be on our way."

I sat down on the folding chair. I could use a bit of rest, too. A while later Asher'ke raised his hand. "Let's get moving."

I helped him get up, put on his battle dress, and tie his shoestrings. He slung his Uzi across his good shoulder, and turned to me. "You grab one too. It's your new friend. Know how to use it?"

"Dad taught me," I said, "but I've never had a chance to fire it. . . ." I picked up the gun with a trembling hand—it was lying near the stretcher—took the pocket flashlight in my other hand, and we moved toward the steps going out. I went first and Asher'ke followed, holding on to me. I turned the flashlight off as I reached the head of the stairs, and we peered out. The night air was cool, and not a sound came from the yard.

"Yep, I think we'll make it," Asher'ke muttered. "Hold on, though," he added, half staggering toward the flagpole at the center of the yard. What could he be doing? I asked myself, but I soon had the answer. With one hand, he drew the drooping flag up to the top of the pole, and made the rope fast. "There," he said briskly. "That's much better. Come on, let's move."

Just then the sound of a tractor came from the direction of the road. I froze stiff. Asher'ke whispered, "Come, we'll go through the field. I know the path among the mines, and it's much shorter."

We headed for the field. I tried to help Asher'ke, but he wouldn't let me. "I can make it on my own now," he said. "If I need help, you can be sure I'll ask for it. Right now, follow me exactly."

Sheltered by the darkness of the night, we plodded ahead. Despite his wound, Asher'ke kept going on his own. That night I learned what the will to live means; it gives a person strength he never knew he had.

It was a long walk. I don't remember what time it was when we finally got to the farm. The important thing is that we made it. We went into the yard and locked the gate behind us. Nicky greeted us with happy leaps and bounds.

It was good to be home again. I opened the main valve for a moment, filled the tea kettle, and put it on the stove to boil. We sat in the candlelight, shutters closed tight and curtains drawn. We gulped the hot tea down and listened to the reports: The enemy had been checked in the north and south. I felt my body going limp with fatigue.

"Now let's try a nap," Asher'ke said, rising.

"You don't think we ought to take turns standing guard?" I asked, like the grown-up I felt.

"No, Nicky will watch over us, without a turn," Asher'ke said. "But to be on the safe side, we'll lock the doors."

That done, we checked the windows and shutters, and pushed the table against the entrance door. It wouldn't stop a tank, of course, but it was better than nothing. At long last we went to sleep—I in Mom's bed and Asher'ke in Dad's. We didn't undress, but even though we were weary, we couldn't fall asleep. Sleep, as they say, was beyond us. But then, how could one sleep after the kind of day we'd had? I lay on my back, and all the sights and sounds kept flashing in my head. I heard Asher'ke, talking as if to himself: "Who would've believed it? Who would've believed it? . . . Sure, we got the alert message in the morning. We put on full gear and got our weapons ready. They said we might have a local clash, but we didn't get excited. We're used to clashes. But that attack, a real hell—"

"I heard it," I said into the darkness.

"At noon we went up to the southern lookout post. That's a nice place when things are quiet, but I don't care if I never see another day like this. At two o'clock I spotted their tanks moving west. I ran over to Captain Zerubavel and said, in a kind of shaky voice, 'Look, twenty tanks are heading this way.' He didn't say a thing, just looked at me with his green eyes, grinned from ear to ear, and said, 'So what's the big excitement, Asher'ke? Have a look *over here*!' I looked and saw twenty more tanks moving westward. Then—and you won't believe it—all of a sudden I felt calm. His cool rubbed off on all of us."

"Captain Zerubavel is a great guy," I agreed. Now I understood that Asher'ke was simply trying to get things out of his system. He talked about how horrible it was to be in the lookout and see them come on, like waves, one mass after another, to see the others firing and firing, vainly trying to halt the charge; how they sat deep in the bunker and learned to tell between our booms and their booms; how they waited for help, then Amiram was hit by shrapnel, right next to him, and never got up; how he himself was hit in the shoulder and remained behind, as the others got into the tanks for the battle.

"Were you scared?"

"Don't know. Maybe. It's natural, right? But if I was scared, it didn't bother me. Until the others left, we talked all the time, mostly about how we would get out. . . . What about you, Eitan. Were you scared?"

"Sure I was."

"How about now? Still scared?"

"Now?" I said to myself. Was I? "No, I don't think so." That's how I really felt.

Again a tractor engine coughed in the distance, then the sound died away. I kept tossing and turning. I wasn't used to sleeping with my clothes on.

"Eitan," Asher'ke said.

"What?"

"What're you thinking about, right now?"

"About all sorts of things, at one time."

"Like which?"

"Like what Dad would do if they told him where I was, right now."

"What do you think he'd do?"

"That's simple. He'd do everything to come and get me. What're you thinking about?"

"Me? Nothing in particular, unless it's the night I went with Zippi, my girl friend, to the movies in Tel Aviv. I keep wondering if I'll ever have another night like that."

"Sure you will, Asher'ke, old boy," I assured him, trying to be brave as all getout. But the bright city lights seemed so far away, in this darkness—a wild dream that can never come true.

"I think so, too." Asher'ke's voice was almost brisk. "The others'll come back and get us out of here. That's how it's got to be."

And so we lay there, in pitch blackness, like two brothers, facing the same fate. Asher'ke may have said more, but I don't remember. I fell asleep.

The Uninvited Guest

Trrrr . . . Brrrr . . . Whoosh . . . Boom!
I don't know if that was the sound that struck my ears, but something like it woke us early in the morning. This time it didn't scare us; we'd known that the fighting would get going again in the morning, right near where we were. Strange how quickly you get used to the new situations you get into. As Asher'ke said: "Man is the kind of animal that gets used to everything."

When I opened my eyes, I saw Asher'ke standing by the window, parting the curtains with his good hand.

"Good morning to you, sir," I said, "and how are you this fine morning?"

"Much better, thank you," he replied, in good spirits.

"See anything?"

"Nothing special. The morning mists are hiding the clouds of war. And what do you see?"

"I see a messed up, wounded soldier," I said, keeping up the fun.

Asher'ke was really something to see. I doubt that his mother would have recognized him. His uniform was crumpled into countless wrinkles, torn here and stained there. The big bandage bulged from under his shirt, his hair was messed as if it had never seen a comb, and his face was covered with rust-colored stubble. But this was no time to worry about the way you looked.

We washed ourselves quickly, then I changed Asher'ke's bandage. The spot was a bit swollen, but Asher'ke assured me that the pain had gone down. We sat down for breakfast, and I tried not to hear the sounds of war coming from somewhere far away.

My friend didn't shut his ears to them. Gulping down the last of his tea, he went over to the telephone and picked up the receiver. "Dead as a doornail," he muttered, replacing the receiver. "Come on, let's go out."

"Where to?"

"Out in the yard. Have a look around."

"Look around for what?" I wanted to know.

"Where we are, fella. You wouldn't want us to

94

sit here in the house, doing nothing, just waiting like prisoners until our luck runs out. Let's go." He picked up his Uzi and went out.

I put the breakfast dishes into the kitchen sink, picked up my Uzi, put the field glasses around my neck, and went out. The little pond in the yard was gone. Only here and there small puddles remained. Nicky came bounding toward us, joyfully but without barking. He understood that this was not the time for it.

We looked in on the coop, the barn, and the stable. The fowl and the animals were in a sorry state. "It does your heart no good to see the cows so upset," Asher'ke remarked. "They're not to blame."

"Nor the chickens," I added.

"Sure, not the horses, either. War is a mean thing."

Most of the troughs still had feed in them. The shells and all that noise must have bothered the livestock. We added fodder here and there, and poured water into the troughs. Asher'ke felt like a real farmer and enjoyed it, and I was caught up with his spirit—for a while, anyway.

A long, unchanging sound came from the main road. Asher'ke looked around. "Is there a good lookout point around here?"

I didn't know exactly what made a good lookout point, and so I also looked around. "How about the barn roof?" I suggested.

"Not bad," Asher'ke agreed. "But what if we have to change positions, kind of suddenly?"

"We'll slide down," I said, laughing at the very idea. But Asher'ke didn't join in. "No, let's get on top of that boulder over there."

I knew the boulder well, of course, and I was surprised that I hadn't thought of it myself. This boulder was flat at the top, and around it was a high growth of Syrian thorns; it was right near the gate. We wiggled through the closed gate, climbed up the boulder, and lay flat, hidden by the thorns. The road was now in clear sight. Perched there, we got the feeling of being in control of what we saw. Asher'ke suddenly began speaking as if he had gone to a finishing school:

"Would you be kind enough to hand me the field glasses?"

"Indeed, kind sir," I replied airily, handing them to him.

"Now will you please come closer to me."

"Yes, commander, sir."

We were so polite—maybe it was a way of relieving the tension. At least, we didn't think it was strange.

I gave the field glasses to Asher'ke. He

scanned the road and pointed. Even without the glasses I could see a long line of trucks winding its way westward, some crammed with soldiers and others covered over with tarpaulin, probably filled with supplies and ammunition.

"That's some caravan!" I whispered. "They must have gotten out all the trucks in Syria."

"Maybe," muttered Asher'ke. "What's eating me is that they're moving with such assurance. If I could do something to the lead truck, or hit the aqueduct, the whole column would be jammed tight."

Just then four planes came screeching overhead.

"I think our air force heard what you said," I remarked.

"Right you are, fella," Asher'ke cried happily. "Just watch them go into action."

One after another, the Phantom jets dived down toward the road. The first two went after the head of the column, which was out of our line of vision, while the others picked other targets. In a few seconds, the entire column, now at a standstill, was wrapped in fire and smoke. Men jumped from the burning trucks and fled away from the road. In a few seconds the smoke became so thick that we couldn't see a thing. It was so awful that I turned away. Asher'ke was moved to recite from the Bible: "And the earth was in chaos. . . ."

I peered at Sugar Valley, Sukri Village, and our lookout post. "Look!" I cried. "Our flag's still up there on the pole!"

"It sure is," said Asher'ke. "That's why they think we're still there, and they'll keep on shelling."

As I looked along the road leading from the post to the farm, I saw something that made me clutch Asher'ke's arm. "You see what I see?"

Asher'ke turned the glasses on the area. "I see something—a cloud of dust rolling toward us." Out of it came a military jeep, twisting and turning among the bumps, and heading toward the farm. I squinted, to see better. No, the jeep was alone, nothing behind it. How many were in the jeep, and who were they—ours or theirs? We had to get ready for the worst.

We hugged the top of the boulder, screened by the bushes, out of sight. At most we were only some twenty yards from the gate. All we could do was keep a tight hold on our guns—and wait.

The jeep came rolling in the dust and halted at the gate. Now we could see clearly that there was only one man in it, the driver. He jumped out of the jeep and went toward the house. Who could he be? All I could see was a figure dressed in a spotted uniform, an army cap, rank straps on his shoulders; at the hip he wore a pistol. He was only about thirty paces away, but I still couldn't tell if he was one of ours or theirs.

What should our move be? I glanced sideways at Asher'ke. His eyes had narrowed and his body was taut. Then, as the uninvited guest began fiddling with the bolted gate, Asher'ke quickly slid down the boulder, straightened up, and pointed the Uzi at the new arrival, crying "Halt!" in English (as he told me later, he didn't know which language he should use—Hebrew or Arabic).

The man at the gate got the scare of his life. I expected him to keel over—he was so scared! At once he raised his hands high, then turned and looked at us. His eyes opened wide. Small wonder! Opposite him he saw a wounded dusty soldier (Asher'ke) pointing an Uzi at him and a youngster not yet eleven years old (me), an Uzi in his hand and field glasses around his neck. As if this were not enough, just then Nicky came bounding out from the house, barking his loudest. The officer looked about for some way of getting out of the situation.

"Halt!" Asher'ke called again.

"Be quiet, Nicky," I called to the dog.

The sound of Hebrew seemed to work magic. A wide grin came to the officer's face. He addressed us, also in Hebrew: "*Shalom,* friends! How are things? I am very, very happy to see you, and, yes, I have very good news for you."

I thought the tone of his voice was kind of strange, like that of someone just arrived from one of the nearby countries. His voice wasn't pleasant, either, but that wasn't important—not if he had good news for us.

As he spoke, the man allowed his arms to drop a bit, but Asher'ke was watching. "Keep 'em up," he ordered, showing the direction with his Uzi.

"But my dear friend," said the other, "I have come to—"

"Up with those hands, or I fire!" Asher'ke advanced toward the man and remained standing about twenty paces away. The officer quickly raised his hands.

By this time I had come down from the boulder. Nicky posted himself by the gate.

"Your pistol," Asher'ke said to the officer. "Throw it down to the ground."

The officer hesitated, then his right hand slid down toward the holster at his hip.

"A little faster," ordered Asher'ke, slapping the side of his Uzi.

The man's fingers were on the holster. Another second, and the pistol was out of its holster. I held my breath. Still another second, and the gun hit the ground with a dull thud.

"And now, my lad"—Asher'ke switched back to our politeness game—"please be so kind as to pick up the gentleman's weapon—and hold on to it."

Nothing to it, eh? Well, at first I was afraid to do it, for some reason. Was I afraid of the man or of the gun? I don't know. But I felt two pairs of eyes on me (not counting Nicky's). I overcame my fear, bent down quickly, and picked up the pistol.

As I was bending down, the officer decided to take advantage of my being between him and Asher'ke to make a dash for the jeep and get away. But a short burst from the Uzi caused him to change his mind; three bullets hit the earth quite close to his feet. He stopped short.

Nicky barked loudly as a flight of warplanes passed overhead. Muffled noises of explosions kept coming from far away.

"Just stand there and don't move," Asher'ke said to the officer. "You'll be better off if you listen to me. Got it?"

The other made no reply. Still keeping an eye on him, Asher'ke said to me, "And now, won't

101

you be a good fellow and open the gate?"

I opened it wide.

"Good boy," said Asher'ke. "You go in first, Eitan, my lad, then you, dear sir, and step on it."

I shut the gate, leaving the jeep on the other side.

"And now, in the same order, we go into the house," Asher'ke went on. "You first, Eitan, then our friend here, then I." We entered the guest room, and Asher'ke locked the door. "Won't you have a seat?" he said, with a broad sweep of his hand.

As our prisoner sat down I could see that he was a bit shaken. Asher'ke planted himself firmly in front of the officer and said, slowly and clearly:

"Your attention, sir. I don't know who you are and why you came here. I can only make a guess. But whoever you may be, you've got no reason to be afraid of us. We're not cannibals, and we don't eat even prisoners. We're all people. All I want to know now is—what's your name?"

"For Thou Art With Me"

As Asher'ke was talking, our captive listened silently, and I was able to take a good look at him. He was about thirty, stocky, of average height, broad shouldered, with a small black moustache decorating his dark, tanned face, and slightly thick lips—a real native, or one born in the region. He moved like a cat, and his eyes blinked a lot. His spotted clothes—well, they might have been enemy uniform or ours. I don't think Asher'ke knew which one.

Both of us knew that the man sitting before us would be a hard nut to crack.

"So what's your name?" repeated Asher'ke.

"Yussef," was the brief answer.

"Yussef what?"

"Yussef Saadon."

"What corps?"

"Armored," he said, blinking.

"Armored? And you're driving a jeep?" asked Asher'ke.

"That's not my jeep. You see, my tank was hit by a shell. I jumped out and had to walk half an hour on foot before I came across this abandoned jeep. I climbed in—and here I am."

"So you are," said Asher'ke. "What else?"

"That's all there is," said the other, blinking.

I found his story a bit strange, but then, so was the whole mess we were in. But why should he have tried to get away from us? What's more—

"You got documents?" Asher'ke went on.

"No."

"An ID tag?"

"No."

"Very strange," muttered Asher'ke, also blinking. "Eitan," he said, "would you be kind enough to frisk the gentleman?"

I had no desire to do the frisking. "I forego the pleasure," I said.

"Can you be moved to change your mind?" suggested Asher'ke.

"How about you changing yours?" I asked.

Asher'ke didn't seem to understand why frisking our captive should be unpleasant, but he didn't press the point. Outside, the echoes of exploding shells reminded us that the war was still going on.

Yussef broke the silence. "How about a drink of water?"

"Sure thing," Asher'ke said, nodding to me. I went into the kitchen, poured a glassful of water from the tea kettle, and handed the glass to Yussef. He gulped the water down thirstily.

"Care for a cigarette?" Asher'ke asked him.

"Very much," replied Yussef.

Asher'ke fished a packet of cigarettes out of his pocket. Something in his eyes told me that an idea had entered his head. He flipped the packet open and extended it to the captive: *"Tfaddal,"* he said to him, in Arabic.

"Ashkurak, many thanks," said Yussef, also in Arabic, drawing a cigarette out from the packet.

Asher'ke seemed to have expected that answer. *"Ashkurak?* So!" he cried out, gleefully. "Arabic comes naturally to you, eh? Just as I thought from the beginning: You are an Arab soldier. A Syrian officer, right? Sure you don't have documents on you? How about handing them over?"

"If you think I'm hiding any, search for yourself," said Yussef, raising his hands.

"So you don't have any," Asher'ke said

crossly. He fell silent, probably racking his brain for another way.

But the new idea was mine. "Say, Asher'ke, maybe he left his papers in the jeep."

Asher'ke stared at me with his glowing brown eyes, and his face lit up.

"Say, you're a pretty smart young man," he said. "How come I didn't think of it?"

"Because you aren't as smart," I replied, grinning. Asher'ke grinned back—but not Yussef. If anything, a black scowl had come to his face.

Asher'ke waited until the roar of planes overhead had died down. The windowpanes rattled, and Yussef made a move as if to duck under the table.

"Now, my dear friend," Asher'ke said, once he could make himself heard again. "Since the idea is yours, how about carrying it out?"

"You bet," I cried, jumping up from my chair. I unlocked the outside door, dashed across the yard, wriggled through the gate, and climbed aboard the jeep. For a moment I imagined how good it would be if I could get behind the wheel and drive away, far from the fighting, to Mom in Hadera; Asher'ke could go back home to Bitzaron. That would be great!

But I quickly shook myself free of these thoughts, particularly because I didn't know how to drive a jeep. On the back seat I spied an army kit bag. I sat down and took a look inside. It was crammed with papers of all kinds, plus a folded map. Everything was written in Arabic. I quickly closed the bag, so that nothing would fly out. My heart was already banging like a hammer. It was beginning to dawn on me who our captive might be.

I jumped out of the jeep and ran back to the house, gripping the kit bag tightly. "Got it!" I cried, as soon as I was through the door.

"Lock the door," Asher'ke called out, "and let's see what you've got there."

I handed the bag over to Asher'ke. One hand still holding the Uzi aimed at Yussef, he pulled some papers out, among them a notebook bound in brown, with printing on the outside. It turned out to be Yussef's military passport, with his photograph, signed and sealed, in Arabic.

"Well, my dear Yussef Saadon, what do you have to say now?" Asher'ke asked, pointing to the kit bag.

The two kept their eyes pinned to each other's faces, as if they were trying to stare one another down. But Yussef understood that the cards were stacked against him. "I have nothing to say," he muttered. "It's all written there, in the papers."

"But it's all in Arabic," Asher'ke cried. That, I thought, must have been the wrong thing to say, for Yussef burst into loud laughter, his body shaking; we thought that he must have gone off his rocker. What was there to laugh at? I, in his place, would have cried. But Yussef went on laughing.

"Everything's in Arabic . . . sure thing!" he said, as soon as he was able to talk again. "And you can't read it. Good, very good, excellent! This bag contains secrets which no one should know. Praise be to Allah and glory be to His name! With His help we went forth to do battle, and with His help we shall defeat you and gain back these Heights, which you call Golan. Then we shall capture Falasteen."

"In your dreams," Asher'ke broke in. I kept quiet, wondering where Yussef got the nerve to talk that way. After all, he was our prisoner, and his fate was in our hands.

"Not at all!" Yussef cried. "Just open your eyes and you will see. We have already taken back half of the territory, and tomorrow we'll take the rest. My regiment will be looking for me. Today, tomorrow, it will get here, and then you two will be *my* prisoners. I might as well start now. What's your name?" he turned to Asher'ke.

"Asher," said my friend crossly. Yussef's words seemed to have taken some of the starch out of him.

"And yours?"

"Eitan," I said. "And what's yours?"

My question seemed to take Yussef aback. "I've told you," he snapped.

"I mean your real name."

Yussef felt insulted. "Yussef Saadon, as I've told you. I do not lie."

"But you're not in the Armored Corps," insisted Asher'ke. "That's not the Armored Corps uniform."

"Well, that's true, it isn't," said Yussef with a faint smile. I myself was a bit worried; we were making small talk with an enemy officer. Next thing, we'd be pals. "Here, let me explain," Yussef went on, "and you'll see that I'm really a decent fellow. I belong to the armored regiment but I have a secret assignment."

"What kind of secret assignment?" I asked.

"It's secret. That's all I can tell you."

For some reason I was very eager to know this secret, although I didn't know how it could help us. Maybe it's because whenever we hear the word "secret" we get curious about it. But think of it! Here we were face to face with an enemy officer, whose army had started a war against us.

I never dreamed that I would be so close to a Syrian officer and talk with him. He knew Hebrew and didn't seem at all like a bloodthirsty enemy. Cunning, yes, but pleasant. What amazed us was his bold speech, even though his fate was in our hands. But if he was that nervy, maybe we could use his nerve to help ourselves.

"If you have a secret mission or something," I said, "we won't ask you any more questions."

"And we won't torture you," Asher'ke said, with a serious face. "That's not our way of getting information out of people, even prisoners."

Yussef's dark face broke into a grin, followed by loud laughter. "Prisoners, eh! Who's the prisoner? Like I told you fellows, in no time you will be mine."

"You mean you belong to a unit that picks up prisoners?" I asked.

Asher'ke grinned. "What's with you, Eitan?" He laughed. "An officer who rounds up prisoners—that's not a secret assignment." I thought I caught a wink in his eye.

"No, no," said Yussef. "Let me explain. I am an officer in—how do you call it?—Intelligence."

"And for that you have to know Hebrew, of course," I prompted him.

"Intelligence Officer, Eighth Regiment!"

110

Yussef said, proudly. "And this"—he nodded toward the kit bag—"is the secret file of Operation Ramadan."

"Operation Ramadan?" repeated Asher'ke, fastening his eyes on the bag.

"Exactly." He fell silent, and it was my guess that he was debating with himself. As an Intelligence officer he was forbidden to talk to us, but then, anything that would break the tension was welcome. Besides, he was so cocksure that soon we would be his prisoners that he allowed his tongue to run loose.

"Ramadan," he said, lowering his voice, "is the name of this operation. I had a hand in planning it, together with the operations officers. I was born here, in Kuneitra, and I know the area like the palm of my hand. I marked the roads that our tanks were to follow; it's shown on the map here. Today I was with my regiment, on this route, when I suddenly found myself looking at this farm, which I had never seen. And so I said to myself, 'I'll go take a look.' I borrowed a jeep and here I am," he ended with a sigh.

"The name of this place," I said, "is Neot-Golan."

"Neot-Golan?" The name seemed to ring a bell. "Neot-Golan—somewhere I've come across the name. Did I hear it? No, I read it in one of your newspapers." He thought hard, then slapped his forehead. "Of course! The tiniest school in the world . . ."

"Some memory!" I said, a bit admiringly.

"And you're looking at the one and only pupil," Asher'ke said, nodding.

"This is my dad's farm," I said proudly.

"Was," Yussef corrected me. "It *was* your father's."

"It was and will be," I shouted.

At this point a thunderous roar of shelling shook the panes.

"That's that," said our prisoner, rising. "That will be my regiment, on its way here."

Asher'ke gave him a side look. "Don't hold your breath," he advised Yussef. "The booming you hear is made by an Israeli Sherman cannon. I can tell the booms apart, and I don't have to be an Intelligence officer to do it."

Yussef drew himself up. "A good Intelligence officer," he said, "must be familiar with more important matters." Then he slumped back into his chair.

Asher'ke glanced at his watch. "Quarter to one. Eitan, my dear, is it within your ability to prepare a light repast for three?"

"For you, Asher'ke, my dear, I shall do my best," I replied and headed for the kitchen. The

112

refrigerator, I found, had been well stocked by Mom before she left—hard-boiled eggs, cold chicken, vegetables, fruit. Mom must be worried about us, I thought, down in Hadera. She might have tried to call on the phone. I worked quickly and tried to think of other things. I placed the full plates on a tray and took it to the dining room.

"Is this food kosher?" the prisoner asked.

"Nothing but," I said.

"First time in my life that I'm eating a kosher meal," Yussef said.

"Don't let it spoil your appetite," muttered Asher'ke. He laid the Uzi across his knees and switched on the radio. Yael Ben-Yehuda was the newscaster, and she reported that our forces had been able to check the enemy in the north and the south. Chaim Herzog, the military commentator, said that the reserve divisions were grouping; some were already at the fronts, and the decisive moment was approaching.

"Sure hope so," I commented, but the other two were silent. As the radio went on, they exchanged rapid glances; they were as much in the fighting as though they had been on the firing line.

I took the dishes back to the kitchen to wash them. Asher'ke had a quick look around the house and came back to Yussef. "I'm afraid we'll have to lock you in," he said. "You'll be comfortable, but don't try to get out. The windows are barred, the door will be locked, and outside there's a dog who can smell a stranger a long way off and do something about it. O.K., come along." He showed Yussef to the north room—mine. That meant that the prisoner would spend the night in my room, among the things I liked best: my books, games, stamp collection. Suppose . . . "Asher'ke," I whispered.

"What's up?" he wanted to know. My voice must have told him that I had an idea stirring in my brain.

"How about checking his pockets?" I whispered again (but it seemed to me that Yussef heard me).

Asher'ke nodded. "If you don't mind," he began.

"Sure, sure," Yussef said sharply (now I was sure he did). From his pockets he drew a wallet, a handkerchief, a cigarette lighter, a packet of cigarettes.

"Thanks," said Asher'ke. "Just leave the lighter on the table."

"The lighter?" demanded Yussef. I could well understand him; how would he be able to light a cigarette without it?

114

"Just a precaution," said Asher'ke.

Yussef was plainly annoyed. "I promise you that I won't try to burn the house down, if that's what's bothering you. Look, if I give my word, I keep it."

Ricky had taught me a saying: "Respect and suspect." But I also remembered another: "Fortunate is he who believes." I chose the second. "I believe you," I said.

Asher'ke handed him the lighter. Yussef slipped it into his pocket, walked to the bed, and said, "You may lock the door."

"If you need anything, knock three times," Asher'ke said, and locked the door behind him.

As soon as we were in my parents' room, I asked Asher'ke the question I'd wanted to ask for some time. "When did you begin to suspect that Yussef is a Syrian?"

Asher'ke slumped down to one of the beds. "Almost from the very beginning," he said.

"How come?"

"The jeep, first of all. Then his hat, then a kind of funny feeling." His voice began to trail away, and his hand moved toward his wounded shoulder.

"What's the matter, Asher'ke?" I cried.

"It's nothing," said Asher'ke hoarsely. "Only my wound." The last hour had been pure agony for my big friend, but he had managed not to show it. "Does it hurt badly?" I asked.

"Like knives cutting into you," he replied. "Would you have anything against pain?"

"Pills?"

"Anything, just to kill the pain." Asher'ke was biting his lips to keep from groaning. He was beginning to feel chills, and I felt them too. I drew a chair up to the tall medicine cabinet, and ran my eyes across the jars and packets until I found a pain killer, Rocal. Asher'ke washed two pills down with one gulp of water and sank back on the bed. I was awfully upset to see my friend in pain; no friend should ever be hurting. What's more, Asher'ke had to be strong, given the spot we were in. It came to me that Yussef mustn't know how sick Asher'ke was. As I looked at his face, I felt myself almost going limp. And come to think of it, I never could stand the sight of anyone in pain. I thought how brave some people were, to be able to hide their suffering, and I always prayed I would never be put to that kind of test. I suddenly recalled a story I had written for Ricky in class: One day I found a magic wand that healed any wound over which it was passed, and soon I removed all the pain and suffering in the world.

But here was my friend Asher'ke, big and

116

strong, yet his body racked with pain because of the shrapnel in his shoulder—and I had no magic wand. He lay there, silent, and I sat at his side, also silent. I thought I should ask him how he was feeling, but I could easily see. Only now and then a faint groan would escape from his lips. I admired him for it; I, in his place, would have been yelling and screaming and calling for my Mom by now. The very thought filled my eyes with tears. I went over to the window and stood there until my tears dried, watching the sun going down to meet the horizon, wondering why the Golan should be wrapped in smoke.

Yussef knocked on the door only once. He wanted to go to the bathroom, and he asked for a book, in English. I found a James Bond paperback on the shelf. He went back into the room, and I locked the door behind him.

More minutes went by—maybe half an hour. The falling dusk crept in through the window, spread to the corners of the room, then filled it completely. Asher'ke's eyes were on the ceiling, as he lay there, flat on his back. His face was blurred in the dark, but I knew that the pain had not gone away.

"Eitan!" he called, and I heard a tremor in his voice.

"Yes, Asher'ke?"

"Would you get me a cover?"

I didn't feel cold, but I spread a woolen blanket over him.

"Thanks very much. . . . By the way, do you have a Bible here?"

"Do I have what?" I repeated, wondering if I'd heard him right.

"Do you have a Bible?"

I didn't know why Asher'ke should have suddenly thought of the Bible, but I went to the bookshelf and came back with the Bible, in the fancy silver binding which Mom got on her high-school graduation.

"Read me something," Asher'ke said as I sat down at the foot of the bed.

"What should I read?"

"Not important, what. . . . Main thing is to read something, O.K.?"

I was a little confused by Asher'ke's request. Could his mind have been damaged by the fever and the tension? Now, of course, I understand it very well. During those painful hours Asher'ke's mind must have shuffled many thoughts—man's fate, death, the war which had broken out just on Yom Kippur, the kind of thoughts that made him want to listen to what our ancient Book had to say. He no doubt felt that by listening to its verses he would be able to draw the courage to endure the pain.

I opened the Bible to the Book of Psalms, at random, and my eyes skimmed over the large letters. I breathed deeply and began reading, softly:

> *A song unto David. The Lord is my shepherd; I shall not want. He maketh me to lie down in green pastures; He leadeth me beside the still waters. He restoreth my soul; He guideth me in straight paths for His name's sake. Yea, though I walk through the valley of the shadow of death, I will fear no evil, for Thou art with me; Thy rod and Thy staff, they comfort me. . . .*

I finished reading the psalm, and the book remained open on my knees.

"Thanks, Eitan. Would you mind reading it again?"

I rose, lit a candle, put the candlestick on the night table, and again read the ancient words. Asher'ke's eyes were closed now, his face was contorted with pain, but he whispered along with me: "Yea, though I walk through the valley of the shadow of death, I will fear no evil, for Thou art with me."

With nightfall, Asher'ke's condition became worse. I tried to change the bandage, but the shoulder was awfully swollen, and the lightest

touch made Asher'ke groan with pain. His forehead was on fire, and I gave him two more pills. That's all I could do for him.

Even now I can't describe how we passed that awful night. I kept my eyes on Asher'ke for a long hour, and felt the tears streaming down my face. I saw Asher'ke in pain, and there was nothing I could do. I felt so little, so helpless.

"Anyone Alive Here?"

I must have fallen asleep quite late, but I got up with the sunrise. Asher'ke was still sleeping, lying on his back and breathing heavily. Not a sound came from my room.

I got up noiselessly, like a thief, washed my face, drank orange juice straight from the bottle, picked up the Uzi, and went out.

An early autumn sun greeted me. In the far distance the roll of explosions echoed in the air, but I paid no attention to it. Jets were streaking across the sky to the north, and I ignored them, too. I simply wanted to enjoy the fresh morning.

Nicky ran up to me and joyfully rubbed his nose against my leg. The animals in the barn and stable looked at me with sorrowful eyes. I could almost guess their thoughts; I had always taken good care of all their needs, and now I had suddenly abandoned them. I patted Roxy on the back and whispered, "It'll be all right . . . it'll be all right." Over by the chicken coop, a rooster was announcing the new day. I knew that everything had to be attended to, otherwise the farm would be ruined. But I didn't have the strength to do it all. I hoped, even prayed, that by some miracle someone would show up and come to help me. Maybe Asher'ke would get up from bed and say, "Everything's in order. No pain. Let's get to work." Or maybe Dad and Albert would roll up in the truck and say, "Let's go, Eitan. It's all a dream."

But it was no dream. Here were the torn electrical wires, and over there the damaged roof, the puddle blots, the slanting electrical pole. All of this reminded me of what had been going on here for the last two days.

I stood in the middle of the yard. A light morning breeze ruffled my hair. I looked about as I always had, in those faraway days of quiet. The loquat and apricot trees were shedding their leaves, and on the pomegranate trees the fruit was beginning to ripen. I suddenly felt an awful urge to go out to the fields and see the coming of autumn, as if this were a peaceful morning.

I wriggled through the closed gate, went by

the Syrian jeep, climbed up the boulder, and scanned the trail leading to the field. The squills stood tall and white; among them the leaves of the crocus peeped out brightly. There were no birds in the sky, and in the east, the oak tree was wondering why I hadn't been coming to visit it.

Just before I climbed down from the boulder, I gave a last look toward the juncture of the dirt road and the main highway, and my blood froze. I gripped the Uzi more tightly. Was I seeing something, or was it my imagination? A single jeep had turned off the highway and was now churning up dust on our dirt road. This jeep looked very much like the one standing near the gate. No, I wouldn't allow it to draw near. But draw near it did. I sprawled out flat on the top of the boulder, hidden by the thorns, and kept my eyes on the galloping jeep. As it came closer I saw that its sides had been camouflaged with mud. It slowed down to avoid a shell hole in the road, then put on speed. Was this jeep carrying soldiers to rescue Yussef? If so, they'd immediately recognize their comrade's vehicle by the gate; we had been foolish not to have hidden it. But then, it would have been found anyway.

As I strained my eyes, I could see one thing: In the jeep was only one person, its driver. Thank goodness for that! My fingers moved toward the safety catch on the Uzi. Of course, the only gun I had ever handled was a toy popgun, but if I had no choice I would pull the trigger, or at least pretend to. "Just keep a stiff upper lip, Eitan," I kept telling myself. "Don't do anything half cocked!"

In the meantime the approaching jeep had skirted the parked one and come to a halt six feet from the gate. A tall fellow got out. He was in battle dress, with a fur-trimmed collar, paratrooper boots, a pistol in a holster at his waist, and dark unkempt hair. For a moment I thought that he reminded me of somebody. He drew near the gate, and as he began fiddling with the bolt, I gripped the Uzi tightly, closed my eyes, and prepared to pull the trigger. "This is it!" I said to myself—but my fingers didn't move.

The newcomer cupped his lips and shouted, "Hello! Anyone alive here in this lonely place?"

The voice was deep and warm, and suddenly my heart was filled with delight.

"Yes, there is!" I shouted, sliding down the boulder.

The driver turned around, his hand moving by habit to the holster. As soon as he saw me his hand dropped to his side. "You? What are you doing here?"

I skipped up and down, now that I had recognized the stranger—Tziyon, Dad's good friend—Tziyon Harari, the scout patrol commander in Dad's unit; he had been wounded in the Sinai Campaign and was now running a cattle ranch in Western Galilee. But, as Dad often said, "once a scout, always a scout." Tziyon never let an opportunity go by to attach himself to a patrol trip, near and far, or go by himself. He scouted little-known areas in Sinai, crisscrossed the Jordan Cleft, climbed Mount Hermon. People said that he had even explored the ghost city of Petra. He also used to pop in on Neot-Golan, usually on Passover or Succot. He would tour the farm, praise us for the way we were taking care of the livestock, compliment Mom on her baking, and describe, in his quick, lively style, all the exciting places he had visited recently.

"What are you doing here?" Tziyon demanded.

"I live here, remember?" I said. "Now how about telling me what you're doing here."

"It's a long story," he said. "Are your folks at home?"

"Why, none of them. Mom's in Hadera and Dad has been called up."

"Don't tell me you were left here all alone!" cried Tziyon in dismay.

Suddenly I remembered Asher'ke and our captive. For a moment they had dropped out of my mind. Now I was more frightened than ever. "Come quickly," I said. "I've got a long story too."

Everything now got mixed up: Tziyon and Asher'ke talking about what was going on; my story, how I got left behind; Tziyon telling his story as he bandaged Asher'ke's wound—everyone was talking at once, but I managed to keep the stories straight. This is what Tziyon told us:

"You probably remember that I was wounded in the Sinai Campaign," he began, as he was changing the bandage. "When I left the hospital they gave me two things: my medical classification and my discharge papers, releasing me from reserve duty. Fine, right? But when this here war broke out, I headed for my battalion. Well, they told me, 'Tziyon, go back home. We'll get this thing settled without you.' But I ask you: How could Tziyon Harari stay home when his pals were fighting at the front? Sure, somebody must have gotten the idea that I wasn't fit for combat duty, but I could be useful for other things, like driving, finding new trails, tracking. Well, you know how it is; if you're not called, you go it alone. I sat in headquarters, trying to figure out what I could do, when I heard that the Golan Heights settlements would be evacuated. That, I said to myself, was the job for me, real important."

"What kind of job, for instance?" asked Asher'ke, forgetting his pain for a moment.

"Easy does it," grinned Tziyon. "After midnight I went to my old jeep, smeared it with camouflage mud, and kind of attached myself to a convoy going up to the Heights. We traveled without lights half the night. The column veered off toward the front, and I headed this way."

"That's all there was to it?" asked Asher'ke.

"Who says so?" demanded Tziyon. "During the night I had to avoid all kinds of unpleasant meetings along the road, but let's not go into details."

"But I still don't understand why you had to come here," said Asher'ke, scratching his head.

"What's there to understand?" said Tziyon, pinning Asher'ke's bandage tight. "The people had been cleared from the settlements, right? But the livestock was still there, right? Now you tell me—who was to take care of the animals?"

"Tziyon Harari!" I burst out, I was so happy to see the tall scout; he had risked his life to come all the way here, just to take care of the cows and horses. I felt that my prayers had been answered; from now on it would be all right.

"That's it!" said Tziyon, ruffling Asher'ke's red hair. "How d'you feel now?"

"Much better, honest," said Asher'ke, smiling faintly—for the first time, it seemed, since he had been hit.

"We're mopping up the Heights," Tziyon went on. "The fellows will be here soon, and they'll take you by helicopter to the hospital, straight into the hands of the pretty nurses."

"No kidding!" Asher'ke said.

"You bet. Now let's have a look at your captive and see what's to be done." He unlocked the door to my room and went inside, shook hands with Yussef, and exchanged a few words with him in Arabic. (Yussef had thought that whoever had arrived was going to free him, and you could see disappointment written all over his face.) Tziyon then had a look at the kit bag I handed him, leafed through the documents, studied the maps. "Say, you've latched onto something big here," he said excitedly. "Our Intelligence officer will recommend you for a citation. Do you know how valuable this bag is to us?" He paused to let his excitement die down. "And now, how about a little snack of sorts? You give me the ingredients, and I'll show you how."

Tziyon wasn't wrong. The breakfast he prepared was filling and tasty. Then we went out to the yard and got to work. Tziyon moved about like a real pro, as if he had been living in Neot-Golan for years. He took out two wrenches and a piece of pipe from the toolbox in his jeep, and in no time at all he had the broken water line all fixed. I opened the main valve, and Tziyon quoted gaily: "Bring up water in joy." All the faucets now brought forth water.

"Now let's get on to the cowshed," Tziyon announced. We were greeted by sad moos; the cows hadn't been milked in about forty-eight hours, and their udders were aching. Tziyon attached the milking machines to the generator and got it going ("Hope the cows recover soon, although we might have to treat the udders a bit," he said). In the meantime we filled the troughs and bins.

There wasn't much to do in the stable; it was too bad we couldn't take the horses out for a canter. We spent some time in the chicken coop. Then, as we were coming out, we saw Asher'ke on the porch. He waved to us weakly and suddenly slumped to the ground.

"What's happened to him?" I cried.

"We'll see. Hurry!"

By the time we got to the porch Asher'ke had

managed to drag himself to the wall and lean against it.

"What's going on?" Tziyon asked, putting his arm around Asher'ke's shoulder.

"Right there," cried Asher'ke. "The pain's awful. I don't have any strength left. . . ."

Tziyon put his palm to Asher'ke's forehead. "He's running a high fever. We must get him help. Where's the telephone?"

"The line's broken," I said.

"That's bad, but we may be able to repair it. But first we've got to get him into bed." Together we half dragged him inside and laid him on the bed.

"Do you know how to work the radio?" Asher'ke asked Tziyon, fighting to talk clearly.

"Sure. Why?"

"Maybe you can try getting through to headquarters from our post . . . if it's still in our hands."

"How d'you get to the post?" asked Tziyon.

"I'll show you," I said.

"Fine. Tell me how."

"I'll go with you," I said.

Tziyon wouldn't agree, at first. There was danger, and Asher'ke couldn't be left alone. Then he changed his mind; I not only knew the way to get to the post but also the post itself.

"What d'you say, Asher'ke?" Tziyon asked.

"Both of you go."

"And you'll be alone with him?"

"He'll stay put. But come back right away," Asher'ke said, smiling weakly.

"Let's go, Eitan," said Tziyon. Suddenly he stopped, turned around, and asked: "I forgot the main thing. What's the code of the post?"

"Eagle Four."

"Ray of Light, This Is Eagle Four"

"Hold on to this handle," said Tziyon as he started the jeep's motor. "We're going ahead at jet speed."

He may have exaggerated a bit, but not much. We streaked along the road, and at every curve I thought we'd topple over. I wasn't worried as much about myself as about making contact with headquarters; if we couldn't, Asher'ke's condition would be even worse.

The jeep sped eastward. On the left and behind us rose mushrooms of smoke, accompanied by booms. We were in luck; the road to the post was clear. "You see, if you're on a worthy mission, you won't get hurt," Tziyon said, keeping the accelerator down to the floorboard. We were going like on the expressway. Every minute, we knew, was precious, for us and especially for Asher'ke. At last we saw the yard of the post ahead. There wasn't a soul in sight, but to be on the safe side, Tziyon halted the jeep behind the thick barbed wire. "Wait here," he told me. "I'm going to take stock of the situation." Pistol in hand, he jumped off the jeep and, bending low, dashed into the yard and disappeared through the bunker entrance. I sat and waited. Then I saw him coming out and waving to me. "Come on," he shouted, "and bring along the flashlight."

I reached into the toolbox and found the flashlight, then jumped out and crossed the yard. How different it was from what I had seen on my first visit! The flag was down again. A bullet or a piece of shrapnel must have cut the rope.

"Not a living soul around," said Tziyon. "Come on. We're going to the communications room."

"Half a minute," I said. I ran up to the flagpole, tied the rope together, and pulled the flag up to the top, tying the rope securely, the way Asher'ke had done the other day. Tziyon grinned and helped tie the knot. "That's it!" I said, not knowing that this act was to get us into a mess.

We went into the dark bunker. I flashed the

light along the corridor until we got to the communications room. Tziyon sat down at the microphone and turned the transmitter on. A red bulb lit up before us. Tziyon waited until the transmitter had warmed up, then began broadcasting: "Hello, Ray of Light, this is Eagle Four. Ray of Light, this is Eagle Four calling. Urgent. Over." Without turning away from the microphone, he said to me: "Ray of Light is the code of the nearest Zahal unit I know of." He went back to transmitting, five, six times. And just as I thought that Tziyon wasn't getting anywhere, and that all we would get would be distant hoots and whistles, suddenly a welcome voice came through the receiving set:

"Eagle Four, this is Ray of Light!" The voice seemed surprised. "Glad to be hearing from you. Have you gone back to your post? Over!"

"We aren't all here," answered Tziyon impatiently. "No time for details. I am requesting an ambulance chopper for Neot-Golan. Very urgent. Over!"

For a moment there was silence, then the voice came in again: "Did you say Neot-Golan?"

"Affirmative. Over."

"Very strange," said the voice. "I have it that the farm has been abandoned, in enemy territory. Over."

135

This made me mad. How did they dare . . .
Without thinking, I bent toward the microphone and yelled, "That's not true! Not true!
What do you mean, abandoned! The farm is in
our hands. I mean it!"

Tziyon pushed me away gently. "You've
heard what he said," he told the man at Ray of
Light. "I've got nothing to add. Over."

When the voice spoke next it carried a note of
gladness. "The chopper will be there as soon as
possible. How about more details? Over."

"O.K. We've got one wounded man to be
taken at once to a hospital. We also have a deliv-
ery package which should best not be discussed.
Over."

"O.K., Eagle Four. The chopper will be on its
way. An armored unit will try getting through to
you. Hold tight. Over."

"Thanks. See you. Over."

It was such a thrill to hear the faraway voice
called Ray of Light. It was really a ray of light in
the darkness. Although the farm was ours, it was
good to know that Zahal was worried about us.
Soon its tanks would be here, and, what's more
important, Asher'ke would be flown to a hospital. That sure was a ray of light!

Tziyon turned off the transmitter. "That's it,
fella. Now it's back to the farm."

We made our way toward the exit and could already see daylight, when suddenly two booms sounded outside. The yard was filled with smoke and the walls of the bunker shook.

"What's that for?" wondered Tziyon.

"They're shelling the post," I said.

"That I can see," returned Tziyon. "But why?"

"Maybe they saw us come here."

"Maybe, but not likely. And I don't think they could have located the broadcast that fast."

We took a few steps forward, and again two booms came down, one nearby and the other farther away. I peered into the yard and suddenly understood why we were being shelled. I was very angry at myself. "I know why they're shelling," I said. "It's because of the flag I hoisted to the top of the pole."

"I think you're right," Tziyon agreed. "They must have spotted it through their glasses." He looked into the yard. "Well, they did it. The flag's down again. Now it should be quiet."

He had guessed right. Suddenly there was dead silence.

"Let's get going before they start again," urged Tziyon. "Follow me!" He ran out into the yard, with me hard on his heels, and headed for the jeep. Suddenly we both stopped. The jeep was lying on its side, smoldering, its tires on fire.

"The devil take them," yelled Tziyon. "Look what they did to my jeep!"

"We've got no choice," I said. "We'll have to make it back on foot. It's not far, though."

"Guess you're right," he muttered and turned toward the road.

"No, not that way," I called after him. "I know a shorter and a safer way." In answer to his questioning look, I pointed to a trail. "It goes right through the field."

"O.K.," said Tziyon. "You lead the way."

I kept to the middle of the trail, with Tziyon right behind me, both of us careful not to step in the mined area. I was sure that we'd get to the farm in no time, and that the worst of the war was behind us. How could I know that in a few minutes we would be in the thick of it again? That's how things kept going—full of surprises.

From the post we headed through the large gully that goes on to join Sugar Valley. We got to the next hillock and climbed it quickly, trying to shorten the distance as much as possible, I with my quick steps and Tziyon with his long strides. Here and there I grabbed a sapling or bush for support, until both of us had reached the top.

"It'll be easier from here on in, my lad," said Tziyon.

"You're telling me!" I wanted to reply, but my breath was coming in gasps. We stopped at the top for a moment. Below us stretched the valley. We would now go on to the oak tree at the other end, skirting the black basalt boulders and the thorny undergrowth. The rest of the way seemed clear until, when we were no more than fifteen steps from the gully, everything seemed to explode all around us; a screeching shell sent a shiver through me.

"Down!" cried Tziyon and pulled me with him to the ground. We were lying behind a low stone fence at least two hundred years old. I peered carefully over it and looked out on the field. It seemed peaceful enough, until my eyes swept the eastern fringe of the field.

"Look there!" I cried, pulling at Tziyon's sleeve. "See something?"

"Sure do," said Tziyon.

"Wonder what it can be," I went on, sorry that I hadn't taken the field glasses along.

It sure was strange. Men in uniform were running all over the field, dodging nimbly from boulder to boulder, crouching behind them and darting out again—like the Indians in the film *Hawkeye* that I saw last year. Each of these "Indians" (Syrians, as I learned very soon) was holding a queer-looking suitcase. Who were these men and what were they carrying? At first I thought I was watching a science fiction war. I kept my eyes on the man nearest me, some fifteen hundred feet away. He was running lightly, then crouched behind a bush, took something out of his suitcase, put it to his shoulder, and pulled the trigger. Something shrieked by overhead.

"So that's what they're doing!" muttered Tziyon. "Firing shoulder missiles!"

"On whom?" I asked, frightened.

"On our tanks. Look over there!" He pointed to the western ridge.

I could see the tanks clearly, as they came sweeping toward the east in a wide column stretching across the entire field, big and threatening, their cannon firing shells toward the retreating Syrian armored corps. The mass of steel kept rolling forward, as if nothing on earth could stop it. But even as we watched, a shoulder missile hit the turret of the lead tank. It halted, as smoke came pouring from the inside, but it still managed to pull to one side, so as not to block the way for the others.

"Why don't they go after the soldiers with the missiles?" I wondered. "Don't they see them?"

I thought I was talking to myself, but Tziyon said, "It's not so easy to fire from a tank at soldiers on foot in the open field, but . . . Aha! Hear that?"

"That" was a burst of machine-gun fire from the turrets, spraying the field thoroughly, glancing off the boulders and sending all the soldiers and their suitcases to the ground for safety; some of them never got up again. The tanks kept going, their fire sweeping the entire field and keeping us pinned down as well, no matter how badly we wanted to get back home. We were caught in the middle, like people forced to watch a play—a nightmare, to be more exact.

A burst of bullets whistled by overhead.

"Take care, lad," yelled Tziyon. "Be sure they don't see you!"

He didn't have to say it twice. I clung to the ground, my chin burrowing into the earth. I was irked by our tank gunners—but how were they to know that behind the fence two of their own were hugging the ground? I tried to dig deeper, while every part of my body wanted to get away from the spot.

Tziyon nudged me. "We've got to make a break for the gully," he cried. "Ready?"

"Ready," I said, without knowing if I could make it.

"Follow me!" he ordered, and his tone put new life into me. I picked myself up, turned around, and dashed toward the gully, running faster than I ever thought I could, with Tziyon just one pace ahead of me. I skirted a dark basalt rock. Another twenty feet and we would be rolling down the slope of the gully. Suddenly I felt as if a knife had been thrust into my left arm, near the elbow. Searing pain got hold of the arm and wouldn't let go. What was this—had I been hit by a bullet or shrapnel . . . ? I didn't think of anything but the few steps to the gully. Tziyon and I hit the slope at about the same time. The pain in my arm seemed to have eased up a bit. I looked at my sleeve: it was torn a bit, and around the spot there was a patch of blood, but I didn't say anything.

Tziyon suddenly knew something was wrong. "What happened?" he demanded.

"I don't know. I think I've been hit."

Tziyon didn't ask me if my arm hurt. Instead, he cried, "Can you lift your arm?"

I tried to lift it, and the arm went up without any trouble, though it did hurt a bit more.

"You're a lucky boy," said Tziyon. "It's a surface cut, from a piece of something. Before a week is out you won't know it happened. Can you keep going?"

"Sure thing."

"Let's go, then. And if you need help, don't be ashamed to ask for it."

We walked on along the side of the gully in a northwesterly direction, toward the aqueduct. We tried to make good time, but it wasn't that simple. We kept close to the gully wall in order to stay out of sight—of both the Syrians and our own men. Tziyon kept steadying me, and I needed it. I felt my strength giving out.

After twenty minutes of walking, Tziyon motioned upward. The sounds of fighting were quite far away, and we had to get out of the gully.

We climbed out and looked around. I could have shouted with joy—if I had had the strength: About one hundred yards from us was the dirt road leading to the farm.

"How do you feel now?" Tziyon asked, noting the happy look on my face.

"Fine. We're almost home," I answered.

"Good. Let's keep going."

I did, but I felt myself growing weaker and weaker. This angered me no end; here we were almost home and I could barely drag myself forward. Tziyon reached out and held me by my good arm. We said no more but kept on plod-

ding for another few minutes. At last we were through the gate. I stumbled the remaining steps to the porch, and there I slumped down, between Asher'ke and Nicky.

To Leave or Not to Leave

"Why did it take you so long? I've been awfully worried. . . . Yes, sure, I know why." Those were Asher'ke's first words, as I lay sprawled out on the porch.

Tziyon told Asher'ke the whole story as he helped me get up and stagger into the house—the contact with Ray of Light, the shelling which had set his jeep on fire, the shoulder missiles.

"I could hear the fighting all the way here," said Asher'ke, "and I assumed that our armored corps was mopping up the Heights. I was hoping it would get here, but this is such an out-of-the-way-place."

Tziyon cleaned my wound and bandaged it. "How's it with you and things in general?" he asked.

"So-so," replied Asher'ke. "At times my shoulder seems to be doing fine, and at times the pain's so strong I think I might faint."

"Fainting isn't for soldiers," Tziyon said. "And how's the captive?"

"He's O.K., no problems. But I'd like to get away from here."

Tziyon helped me put on a fresh shirt, then went over to the window and peered into space. "They promised to come real quick."

"I think I hear them coming," I said, more because I was feeling better than anything else.

"And I think you're right!" said Tziyon. By this time, all of us could hear the chugging of a helicopter motor, approaching from the west. We hurried out to the porch, and there we saw a welcome sight: The chopper was heading straight toward us. It seemed to hang in the air, then circled around the farm looking for a suitable landing spot. Finally it came down right in the middle of the yard, exactly between the house and the stable, and its rotor swished the tree branches all around. The motor was cut, and two men came out of the chopper's belly, one a lieutenant and the other, with a folded stretcher, a sergeant. Tziyon and I ran toward them, with Asher'ke behind us and Nicky—his usual self—barking noisily.

148

"Quiet, Nicky," I called to the dog. "These are guests!"

Nicky got the idea and sat down, looking distrustfully at the giant steel bird.

"Hi, there, fellas! Glad to be here," said the lieutenant (I guessed rightly that he was the medic).

"Not half as glad as we are to see you here," returned Tziyon, for all of us. As he led the way inside the house, the officer looked at me, wonderingly: "Say, there's a kid here, too. Major Yoni did say that he heard a youngster's voice over the radio, but I didn't believe him. I'll have to ask his pardon. What's your name, friend?"

"Eitan."

"And I'm Lieutenant Manor." We shook hands gravely. "Call me Doc." He looked around. "Where are the wounded?"

"There's only one, and that's me," Asher'ke broke in. He saw the sergeant unfolding the stretcher and made a move to stop him. "I don't need this thing. If you'll help me, I'll get in under my own steam."

The sergeant snapped the stretcher shut and helped Asher'ke to the helicopter, with Doc alongside. The three clambered aboard the craft, and Asher'ke made himself comfortable on the cot attached to the floor.

Just then Tziyon came out of the house, holding firmly on to Yussef. The captive officer came down the steps wordlessly, and the two went up to the helicopter.

"Who's that?" asked Lieutenant Manor.

"An enemy Intelligence officer," replied Tziyon, "and he should be brought to the staff command as quickly as possible."

"His name is Yussef Saadon," I put in. I turned to him and said: "So who is whose prisoner, sir?"

Maybe I shouldn't have insulted him that way, seeing what his condition was, but the words were out before I could stop them. Yussef gave me a dark look, then, like a panther, he broke away toward his jeep, which was waiting for him on the other side of the gate. He was very daring, very brave.

"Halt!" Tziyon yelled after him, drawing his pistol. We held our breath. That was all we needed, after all our watchfulness, that he should get away.

Suddenly Yussef stopped in his tracks. He had to—the gate was locked, and before he could open it, Tziyon's hand was on his shoulder.

"Why take chances?" Tziyon said quietly. "I could have shot you down, but I'd rather watch over your life and good health. Now be a good fellow, and it'll earn you a visit to Israel, by air."

Yussef knew the odds were against him. He went to the helicopter, past the four of us, and climbed inside. I felt like offering him a word of comfort, but I said nothing.

Tziyon gave me a nudge. "Your turn, pal," he said. "All aboard."

"Who—me?" I asked, in confusion. "Into the helicopter?"

"Sure," he said. "You have to get away from here. This is no place for kids."

"But I—" Tziyon's words had come all of a sudden. I'd never thought about leaving. Then I heard Asher'ke calling from inside the chopper. "He's right, Eitan. You were going to be evacuated, right? The evacuation got all balled up, but this is your chance. Come on aboard!"

Maybe they're right, I said to myself. I'd had enough of this war and all the tension. Enough. I'd leave this place, go be with Mom, rest, sleep, without fear or worry. Tziyon would keep watch over the farm and handle the livestock. Then, too, when would I ever again have a chance to go up in a helicopter. Why not?

"Decide quickly, young man," said Lieutenant Manor. "We must take off. We have other calls to pick up wounded." He climbed aboard and said to the pilot, "Start the motor!"

151

I gave Tziyon a questioning look.

"Don't worry about the farm, pal," he said. "I'll be staying here until your Dad comes back."

I was about to climb in and take off, with Asher'ke and Yussef Saadon, when I heard a familiar sound from the direction of the dirt road. I looked toward it, and what I saw made me run up to the helicopter. "You can take off . . . I'm staying here!"

"What's the idea, pal?" demanded Tziyon. "What happened?"

"Go, go, take off!" I shouted to the pilot.

The rotors went on with a terrifying noise, and the wind from the blades streaked across my face. We retreated to the house, and watched the chopper take off, straight up. I waved to it. Those inside had left us and were on their way away from the fighting, to the hospital, headquarters, where it was nice and quiet. Only the two of us, Tziyon and I, remained here, in Neot-Golan, on the front line.

"Why didn't you go with them?" Tziyon asked again.

I didn't answer. First I watched the helicopter, as it turned into a speck and disappeared, then I turned to the dirt road to listen to the familiar sound. Tziyon had heard it too. "So that's why you didn't want to leave the farm?" he asked, suddenly reading my mind.

"Sure—it's my home, you understand?" I was trembling with sudden excitement. "I didn't leave it when it was being shelled. Why should I leave it when *they* have come?"

"They" were six tanks clanking along the dirt road—our tanks—leaving behind them a long trail of dust. The roar of their engines was like music. Tziyon and I stood there, our mouths open, watching the column roll up to the gate.

"Now you get it, Tziyon?" I shouted happily, keeping close to him.

"I get it, pal," he replied. "Come on. We must open the gate and clear the road." He yanked the gate open, jumped into the Syrian jeep, still standing where Yussef had parked it, started the motor, and drove it to the house. In the meantime the tanks had come right up to the fence, swung their cannon aside, and shut off their motors. One by one the drivers climbed down from their steel monsters and strode toward the open gate, tired, their whiskered faces black with soot, the wounded supported by the others. They looked like war, but to me they meant the end of the nightmare.

"Say, is this Neot-Golan?" the nearest one asked.

153

"You're on the beam," said Tziyon. "Come on in."

"Make yourselves at home," I added, laughing with joy.

"Who's the kid?" someone else wanted to know.

"Just treat him nicely," grinned Tziyon. "He's the boss of this spread, and quite a guy."

One by one they filed through the gate. Their commander, Major Nissim, called out: "At ease—until the next announcement."

The hours that followed were too wonderful for words. The soldiers filled the house, and, as I had invited them, they made themselves at home, sprawling on the chairs or stretching out on the floor. They stroked Nicky's back, washed their faces, drank from the faucet and from the bottles of fruit drinks, then shed their dusty shirts. One of them picked up the telephone receiver.

"Line's broken," I told him. "Must have been torn in the shelling."

"No problem," he said cheerfully. "Hey, Yossi, Itzik," he called. "Let's fix the line and we'll be able to call home."

The three went outside with Tziyon, located the torn wire, fished out some wire and tape from one of the tank toolboxes, and very soon

154

there was a line waiting to use the telephone.

It was wonderful to have them, even though, on an ordinary day, Mom would have said that they were messing up the house something fierce. But this certainly was no ordinary day, and I'm sure Mom would have been delighted.

I sat with them, listening to their stories about the armor-against-armor battle which broke the enemy up. I told them about the farm and how I was left alone on the first day of the fighting. One of them, Elik, had read about the tiniest school in the world, and he asked to see it.

"No problem," I said, speaking in their manner. "Come with me." But as soon as I stepped outside on the porch, I saw a small pickup truck rolling into the yard. *Another guest,* I thought, but right away I felt my heart skip a beat: The truck looked very familiar. The next thing I knew Nicky was streaking past me, barking his head off. I called to him to be quiet, but he barked all the more loudly, joyfully.

The truck came to a halt alongside the Syrian jeep. Out of it stepped a bare-headed soldier wearing a crumpled uniform with the rank of major. He had his back to me, but I needed no more. He turned around, our eyes met, and I yelled, "Dad!" and rushed straight into his arms.

155

Elik stood off to one side, quietly.

It was Dad, all right, my own Dad. But he looked at me as though turned to stone. "You!" he cried, his eyes opening wide.

"Daddy! Daddy!" was all I could say, embracing him with all my might, as if I were afraid he would disappear.

He pressed me close to him. "I hopped over to see what's doing here at the farm," he finally said, his eyes now sparkling with joy, "but didn't have the wildest notion I would find you here, especially today. What are you doing here, son?"

"I'm having a good time with the armored fellows."

"The bus didn't come to pick you up?"

"What bus?" I asked. I'd completely forgotten a bus was to have come here. But Dad didn't understand. "Don't tell me you hid when it came," he said sternly.

"Not at all," I cried, surprised by the thought. "Nobody came, I promise. Only Tziyon—but that was this morning."

"So you were here alone during the two days of fighting?" he asked, frightened.

"This is the third," I corrected him.

I could see that Dad was upset. He looked around the yard and the house, at the soldiers

strolling about, very much at home. He didn't say a word, though.

"Fellows." I heard Yossi's voice. "Out to the tanks for a briefing." The soldiers crossed the yard and headed for the tanks. Dad grasped me around my shoulders and said, "Come inside, Eitan."

We went to the dining room. I felt all choked up, tired and happy all at once. One of the soldiers was still at the telephone. He said a hasty *"Shalom"* and hurried out of the house. Dad picked up the receiver and began dialing.

"Shalom, Tirza," I heard him say to Mom (she seemed to be at the other end of the world). "This is Eitan's dad. . . . Why I am saying that? It's a long story. . . . Yes, he's right here, by my side." He drew me closer to the receiver, and I could hear Mom's excited voice. "Yes, he looks great." He gave me the receiver. "Mom wants to talk to you."

I took hold of the receiver, and whatever was choking me was getting bigger and bigger.

"Hello, Eitan dear," I heard Mom's voice, soft, loving.

"Shalom, M-mom," I whispered and—I'm ashamed to talk about it—I burst into tears, crying like a little boy, unable to say a word.

Abandoned Village

Why should I have burst out crying? That's what
my parents wanted to know. I cried for a long
time, maybe three whole minutes, and I was so
ashamed because I couldn't stop. I sure was
glad that none of the soldiers was around to see
me. What would they have thought?

Mom got awfully frightened when she heard
my sobbing on the other end of the line. Wow!
She was sure I was a mess, just one big open
wound, and Dad had a time trying to convince
her that I was all in one piece (it was lucky that
my sleeve hid the scratch on my arm). Then he
had to convince her that he was all right. Finally
Mom calmed down, and the telephone talk came
to an end.

Well, why *did* I cry? I don't have a straight
answer. Of course, I should have been happy.

Maybe I was, and that's why I cried—feeling happy after three days of fear and tension and danger and everything else I had had to overcome all by myself—looking after the farm, running between the bullets, taking care of wounded Asher'ke, guarding the captive, getting hit in the arm by shrapnel, and all. I don't think there were many kids in the country who had had all these things happen to them. And here Dad suddenly showed up at the farm and I heard Mom's voice—and right then and there I again felt like an ordinary kid of my age. And so I let myself be little Eitan, crying to his parents and waiting for them to pity him. I think that's why I cried; anyway, that's how it seemed to me.

As I cried, I felt the tension lessening, and my heart grew light again. Dad looked at me, a little confused, not knowing what to do except say, "Enough . . . enough." I finally went to the washroom, washed my eyes and face and dried them well, to remove all trace of tears, and went back to the others, just as the door opened and Major Nissim stuck his head into the room. "*Shalom*, Eitan and his dad. We're shoving off."

"*Shalom,*" replied Dad. "Good luck!"

"Where are you headed for?" I asked, thankful that Nissim had popped up when he had.

"You're already at the border, aren't you?"

"That's right," he replied. "But we shall be crossing the border and going on a bit Damascus way. *Shalom*, everybody."

"Wait!" I shouted. I suddenly remembered something and wondered how Tziyon and I could have forgotten it. "Before you go, I've got something to give you."

"Thanks, really, you don't have to," Nissim said. "We've already taken too much, and we're really in a hurry."

"But you don't understand. This is something different." I went over to the chair with the kit bag slung across its back. "See, I found this in the Syrian jeep. Tziyon said you'd be awfully interested in it."

Major Nissim quickly reached for the bag and pulled out the folded maps and other documents. He spread them on the table, and he and Dad bent over them. The more they looked at the markings and drawings, the more excited they became—like children who had come upon a shiny treasure.

"Look, look." Nissim put his finger on a spot on the map. "They have a rear command post here that we knew nothing about."

"And here, along this road, is a minefield," added Dad.

161

"And look at what we've got here!" cried Nissim in amazement, holding up a sheet of cardboard with one word written on it in Arabic, in red (later I was told that it meant 'Top Secret'). "This looks to me like the new communications code of the armored unit we're after!" He took me around the shoulders and said, with shining eyes, "This is terrific, fella! Our job will be a bit easier now, and thanks to all this we should have fewer wounded. If I weren't in a hurry, I'd give you a great big hug."

"It's O.K." I smiled. "Next time."

Kit bag in hand, Nissim was already on the other side of the door, when he suddenly halted. "I almost forgot," he said to Dad. "We like this place. It's out of the way and quite safe. Would you mind if we set up our Tagad here?"

"Sure thing, go right ahead," said Dad.

"What's Tagad?" I wanted to know.

"A battalion station for bringing in the wounded," Nissim explained. He turned to Dad. "I knew you'd agree; the question was just formal. Anyway, the medical crew will get here soon and start setting things up. Hope it won't have anything to do. Now we'll be moving east."

"Commander!" someone called outside.

"Coming," Nissim yelled back. He gave me a

healthy whack on the shoulder and left, on the run.

Tziyon, with Nicky at his heels, came in just as the tanks were leaving. He and Dad embraced each other happily, and the two sat down at the table, like the good old friends they were.

"I think we're beginning to see daylight," Tziyon said. "But those animals really got a raw deal. We make use of them, O.K. But why should they suffer just because we human beings decide to make war on each other and do other crazy things? All right, let's get down to business. I went from the barn to the stable, then to the chicken coop, and I did whatever I could: spread out fodder, milked the cows and collected the eggs. But as soon as you can do it, call in the vet. I think some of the milking cows have udder inflammations because they were milked late."

"Thanks, really, Tziyon," said Dad. "A good angel must have sent you here. Or maybe you're the angel himself! How could Eitan have made it without you?"

"He did all right." Tziyon gave me a broad wink. "But how could I have made it without him? . . . By the way, how's Albert?"

"Yes, how's Albert?" I repeated, angry with myself for letting Tziyon be the first to ask.

Nicky, hearing Albert's name, looked at the door and gave a short bark. Dad didn't answer right away. He lowered his eyes, and I knew that something had happened to Albert.

"He's in the hospital in Safed," Dad said at last. "He was wounded on the second day of the fighting—yesterday, come to think of it. Shrapnel in his arms and legs. But the medics say he'll be out in no time."

I gulped. I couldn't imagine tall, strong Albert lying weak and helpless, with a nurse taking care of him.

"And where were you, Dad?" I asked suddenly. "You haven't said a word about yourself."

"This isn't the time for stories, boy," Dad replied severely. "I was up at the front, like the others. Nothing more."

"Where?" I pressed him.

"In the northwestern sector, not far from here. It was tough . . . very tough. After one hour of fighting we had four tanks left, against fifty of theirs. But we didn't break. We kept them stalled until our reinforcements arrived. What can I tell you, son? War's a terrible thing."

"I know," I sighed, recalling that Asher'ke had used almost the same words. When was it—yesterday, the day before?

164

Night was beginning to cast its shadows. Dad glanced at his watch. "Got to get back," he said, but just then the telephone rang. Dad picked up the receiver, listened, and said words like "all fine . . . give her kisses," after which he told me, "Grandma Lea says they've just taken Mom to the maternity hospital. . . . *Mazel tov.* Good-bye, everyone, and see you soon."

A few seconds later I heard the truck pull away and drive out of earshot. This time I wasn't sad. What's more, fifteen minutes later another car rolled into the yard—an army ambulance, with the battalion's medical crew aboard. The doctor, I was glad to see, was none other than Lieutenant Manor of the helicopter, with a crew of three orderlies. They turned the schoolroom into a gathering place, something like a clinic, near the front. I kept away from the place, even though Lieutenant Manor was my friend. It had a sharp smell of disinfectants and bandaging stuff, and I was put off by the sight of the operating table, the blood transfusion equipment, and the rest. I think I've already said that I can't stand seeing anyone in pain.

It was now nighttime. Tziyon called us for supper. All of us, the Doc and his crew as well, sat around the table, and as we ate, we listened to the Chief-of-Staff being interviewed on the radio. He promised that we would win the war, and said that our boys were fighting like lions. But I already knew that.

The night passed very quietly; if there was firing somewhere, I didn't hear it, I slept so soundly. In the morning I was awakened, as always, by Nicky's barking. What? I asked myself. More guests?

Out in the yard I saw an army command car, heading toward the classroom—the clinic, that is. It brought two wounded soldiers, one with his head bandaged and the other one hurt in his knee. The two gave me broad grins. I stood at the open door but didn't go inside. I heard the following:

Doc: "What's new at the front?"

First Wounded: "Fine. Moving forward."

Second Wounded: " 'Significant progress,' as they say."

Doc: "Where were you hurt?"

First Wounded: "Inside Syria."

Second Wounded: "Please note: inside Syria, not the Golan Heights."

First Wounded: "Unless you mean where—in the head, in the knee."

Doc: "That I know. I was talking geography."

Second Wounded: "Well, we were moving against a village . . . what was its name? . . ."

166

First Wounded: "Sukri."

Second Wounded: "Right. Sukri."

At the mention of the name I rushed inside the room. "Did you say Sukri?" I asked excitedly.

"Sure. So what if we said Sukri?"

"You don't understand. There, in Sukri, I have a friend. That's right," I added, seeing the look of disbelief on their faces. "Before the war he used to come to meet me, in the field. His name is Saleem. He has a donkey name Sussu, and we're friends."

In the meantime, Doc had taken care of the first wounded soldier and had begun treating his companion's knee.

"Say Doc, can I go back to my unit?" asked the first man, feeling around the fresh bandage around his head.

Lieutenant Manor looked him over slowly. "Well, it's a surface wound," he mused. "On the other hand, I'd prescribe a short rest. But if you insist . . ."

"Oh, I insist very much!"

"How about me?" asked the other.

"You stay put today," the Lieutenant said, "and you can insist all you want." He turned to the orderly. "We'll give him local anaesthesia."

"Let's get going, Levi," the command-car

driver said to the first man. The two turned to go, with a word of thanks, and I went with them to the command car, all the time thinking about my friend.

"How are things in Sukri?" I asked the driver.

"Nothing special," he replied. "A village like all villages on the Golan, rutted roads that chew up the tires."

"It's abandoned," added the wounded soldier. "Makes you feel kind of sad."

As they climbed aboard, I spoke the question that had been on the tip of my tongue. "How about my going with you?"

"To Sukri?" wondered the driver.

"Yes. Can I join you?" My arm was already resting on the jeep.

"Well, Levi," demanded the driver. "You heard the man. What should we tell him?"

"Tell him to hop aboard, and that's it," said Levi. "The kid deserves it."

"And how is he going to get back?" persisted the driver.

"Plenty of cars on this route. He may even go back with you."

"If worse comes to worst, I go back on foot," I said. "It's not that far." With that, I waited no more and hopped aboard the command car.

I told Tziyon where I was going, and two minutes later we were on our way east, bumping along a road churned up by tank treads. But I didn't mind. Until now I had seen Sukri only from afar, wrapped in a light blue haze, because Saleem used to cross to our side of the border to meet me. Now there was no more border, and I was on my way to Sukri, past the smoking wreckage of an enemy tank, and on inside the village.

The command car rolled along the main street of the village—a dirt road pitted with holes. The stillness of death hovered above us. The shutters of the squat stone houses were tightly closed. At first, the only sign of life was a bony dog dragging himself slowly across the road and sniffing the heavy dust. Farther on two brown hens were pecking away. At a doorway a few paces farther, two wizened old men were squatting on the ground. They stared at us blankly as we came up, no trace of interest on their wrinkled faces. Nothing, I thought, could ever surprise them.

"This is where Saleem was born," I said to myself. "This is where he lives."

Suddenly I felt very lonely. Had it not been for one of our tanks in the village square, its turret open and its commander in position, I would have sworn I was in some ghost town. At a fork in the road the driver veered to the left, and I kept scanning every house, every window, every yard. Suddenly I saw something familiar. "Can you stop for a second?" I asked the driver.

"What's up?" he asked, stepping down on the brake.

"Just one second," I repeated, keeping my eyes on the familiar sight: a small donkey, sad-eyed, his ears lowered.

"Just for a second, then. We've got to move on."

I jumped off the command car and ran to the courtyard. The little donkey glanced at me, wagged his tail, and went on with his thoughts. A white-haired old man opened the door and peered at the strange sight of an Israeli boy in the village.

"Marhaba," I greeted him in his tongue. "Perhaps you know Saleem?"

The old man said he did.

"Would you know where he is now?"

This he didn't know. There had been much excitement when the Israeli forces had entered the village the night before, and no one knew who had run away and who was still there. Only a few had stayed—that he knew.

I didn't know what to do. Everything was so still—the houses, the old man, the donkey.

170

Should I try the alleys, look into the yards for my friend?

"Come on, fella," urged the driver. "Let's go."

"One last second," I begged, desperately looking about. Then, just as I was about to go back to the command car, I heard a thin, hesitating voice behind me.

"Eitan?"

"Saleem!" I called happily, turning around.

Well, there was Saleem, looking as I'd always seen him—thin, barefoot, his hair in knots, dressed in a long raggedy shirt and worn pants. I knew he was glad to see me, but his face was very sad and there was fear in his eyes.

"*Shalom*, Saleem," I said. "How are you?"

"I am well," replied Saleem, his eyes fixed on the command car and the soldiers in it. "How goes it with you?"

"You see? I came to visit you."

I was so glad to see that the war had not come between us. The fear in his eyes disappeared as he looked at me. Sure, he was frightened by the sight of Levi, all bandaged up; and it was because of our army that the villagers had abandoned their homes. But if the grown-ups fought one another, maybe we, the youngsters, could live in peace, borders or no borders.

"We're moving on, fella," said the driver.

But now I didn't want to move on. I had nothing else to look for. I had found Saleem and wanted to be with him for a while. "You can go on. I'm staying."

"Come on, cut it out," the driver called, reaching out for me with his hand.

A car came toward us from the direction of the front, its green color hidden by layers of dust. A sticker on its windshield said ON DUTY. Three men were inside. The car drew up and stopped.

"See those two kids?" one of the men called out. "One looks like a Syrian and the other like an Israeli—"

"You're right!" said another. "And what's more, that Israeli youngster looks familiar."

I looked at the one who said I looked familiar. He was wearing a neat uniform with "Military Correspondent" on the shoulder straps. He looked familiar, as well; but who could he be and where could we have met? Only on the farm, of course. Then I remembered. He was the TV reporter who had come up to do a piece about the tiniest school in the world. With him in the car were the cameraman and the sound man.

"*Shalom*, TV!" I called.

"Look who you meet here!" the writer exclaimed. "Who'd have thought we'd meet here?"

"Tiny world, isn't it?" I said. "Just like the school."

"Hey, wait a minute, Gil," the cameraman said. "Is this the kid the Major was telling us about, the one who got those Syrian war plans?"

"None else," said Gil. "Let's interview him."

They climbed out of the car. I introduced my friend: "This is my pal. His name is Saleem."

To make a long story short, the command car went on its way to the battalion, and the TV people made good use of the opportunity to tape a story about "the flourishing friendship between a Syrian boy and an Israeli boy, in an abandoned Syrian village on the firing line." You may have seen it.

Gil stood at my side and talked—to me, to the camera, into the mike. "Well, Eitan," he said, after the interview, "I suppose you'd like to hitch a ride with us to the farm."

"Sure," I said, "but—" I looked at Saleem. He looked at us, and suddenly began talking into the microphone (in Arabic, which Gil later translated): "What will happen to me now? I have no parents here. I have no one. All of them were afraid and ran away. We were always told:

'The Israeli soldiers are bad and cruel. If they come here, that will be the end of you.' But I said: 'That isn't true. They won't do anything to you. I know them.' They didn't believe me and ran away. But I stayed in the village, with a few of the elders and my donkey. . . ."

His voice was sad. Then he stopped. We too were silent. Only the camera kept grinding away. (By the way, this part was not shown on TV.)

I came closer to him and said, "You want to come with me, Saleem? Come . . . until your parents return."

"And Sussu?" he asked, putting his arm around the donkey's neck.

"You didn't think we'd leave him behind, did you?" I grinned.

He grinned back, and the TV fellows laughed loudly. A minute later we set out for home—a small strange caravan on a road torn up by shell fire and tank treads, a car bumping along, followed by a small, sad-looking, but sure-footed donkey.

Life Is Full of Surprises

Well, I'm almost at the end of my story. Just a few things left to keep the record straight.

The war kept moving away from us. The armored columns set the border at Mazraat Bet-Djan. A few days later Lieutenant Manor came up to us on the porch with good news: "Good luck! There's a cease-fire!"

Everything all around seemed to drop into peaceful quiet. Soon several things happened which should be told, even briefly.

First, the battalion clinic left us. The doctor and his orderlies put the medical equipment into the ambulance, said "*Shalom*—see you on happier occasions," and headed for some point nearer to the border. The one most sorry to see them leave was Saleem; after the Doc had removed a small growth from the nape of his neck, Saleem thought he was a magician, if not Allah Himself.

On the next day Dad got his release from the army. "They decided that here, in this outlying settlement, I would be as useful as in my unit," he said. He took off his uniform and put on his work clothes. He and Tziyon toiled from morning till night, putting the farm back into shape. That was really hard work; Dad remarked one evening, "I am more worn out here than in the army." And I said, "We'd rather you be here, in work clothes, than there, in uniform with ribbons." He fully agreed with me.

A day or so later Saleem went back to his village. Major Nissim came especially to tell us that the villagers who had fled from their homes were now permitted to return. He invited Saleem to come along in his jeep, but Saleem wanted to go back on foot, with his Sussu. I went with them to the oak tree and said, "Now that there's no border and no war, we'll be able to visit each other any time we want." But for some reason we didn't see one another often. At times he'd come during my lesson (yes, after the Succot holiday the schoolhouse opened again, as you will see), and I'd invite him to sit there and listen. He may have learned something; I never tested him.

Then Mom came home and was happy to see me safe and sound. She didn't come all by herself, of course; little Shlomit was with her. Shlomit is my little sister. Dad says she was given that name for Grandpa Shlomo, but Mom says that the name, taken from *"shalom"*—peace—means that we and Shlomit will live together soon in peace. Shlomit is still an infant, and I can't tell if she's pretty or not or whom she looks like most. At night she wakes me with her whimpering, and that's when I get angry with her. But during the day, when she looks at me with her big laughing eyes, I suddenly find I'm crazy about her. I'm not ashamed to write that. After all, she *is* my sister!

Next came a long line of visitors, all kinds of relatives and friends. Grandpa Yehuda came from Hadera, "to get a first-hand account"—my story, that is— "of what happened here during the war." He declared that I did the family tradition proud, and told me, "Now, Eitan, you'll surely want to come with me, spend a week in the colony, sleep, rest, see movies. . . ." But I said, "Thanks, Grandpa, really, but I don't need entertainment. I think I'm still needed here."

Well, Grandpa Yehuda looked disappointed, but he didn't say anything. I guess he felt that my answer was also in the family tradition. Grandpa is a wise man.

Every two or three days another car would roll into the yard—some large, some small—with a guest or visitor: a representative of the Jewish Agency, to appraise the damage caused by the shelling; a representative of National Insurance (my parents had to sign forms in order to receive compensation); a photographer; a busload of tourists from America who came to tour the battle lines and be inspired to buy more Israel Bonds.

One day a Willys truck came into the yard and from it alighted—yes, Albert, none other. His foot was in a small cast and in his hand he carried a cane. All of us were happy to see him back, but Nicky almost went crazy with joy. I had to hold him back with all my strength, to keep him from toppling Albert over. "That's all I need now," Albert grinned. "A third wound. Believe me, two are enough."

On the following day we walked out with the cows to the field opposite Sugar Valley, and I had the feeling that the good old days were coming back.

Well, Albert had come back, and now Tziyon

left us to return to his own farm in Galilee. It was a bit sad, parting from him; I think he was the saddest of all.

Another guest I loved to see back again was, of course, my teacher Ricky. She arrived one early morning, in Sergeant Nimrod's jeep. Both of us were excited to see each other, and there were hugs and kisses, until Nimrod broke in jokingly: "Come on, Ricky, make up your mind—it's him or me. . . ."

Ricky told me that when the fighting broke out she returned to her unit and served as Education Sergeant in a reserve battalion. Now she was permitted to come back to Neot-Golan, and she was to teach me until the new teacher came. For that alone I was ready to give her another hug. But first we had to clean the classroom, so instead of being a teacher and a pupil we were two cleaning people. Then we went back to our studies—not an easy matter; the war was still all around us, and, also, I had to help Dad and Albert every now and then. Ricky understood me well. Besides, it wasn't easy for her, either, to go back being a teacher in peacetime.

"These days have taught all of us a lesson in living," she said. "Now, Eitan, we must learn how to live life as usual." I think she was very wise.

Then came the last surprise. This was on a rainy November evening, a month after the war. It was bitter cold outside, and the dirt road was full of puddles which glistened in the waning light of day. A car drove into the yard and came to a stop near the porch. Two figures got out— a young man dressed in khaki and a boy my own age.

My heart jumped with joy. The young man was Asher'ke—as likable as ever, his shoulder almost all healed. With him was his younger brother, Ami. After we were done with the greetings, the questions and answers, Asher'ke came straight to the point.

"What I'm going to ask may sound strange," he began. "When I spent time here, before the war and even more during the war, I fell in love with this place. In the hospital I thought a lot about it, and suddenly I decided that I would like to live here, in Neot-Golan, for a while, about a year, let's say—work on the farm, go out to pasture, keep watch, anything. During this year, I'd decide what to do later on. My brother Ami could be with me; he could live with Eitan, go to school, work and play, even fight. Why not? It's healthy. . . . Well, that's enough from me. Now I'd like you to give me an honest answer. Would you want to have us?"

Dad and Mom exchanged wondering glances and didn't know what to say. I looked at Ami. I liked him from the minute I saw him; no wonder—he was Asher'ke's brother, wasn't he? I wanted very much to have him on the farm, but I didn't want to say anything before my parents had spoken.

But it was Albert who broke the silence. "What's there to discuss?" he said. "Let's put out the welcome mat for Asher'ke and Ami. Asher'ke will begin working on the farm tomorrow. We have plenty of work and that's good for the appetite. You, Asher'ke, will sleep in my room; after all, both of us are wounded soldiers." He gave Asher'ke a resounding whack—right on the wounded shoulder!

Since then, Asher'ke and Ami have been living with us on the farm, and we're now one great big family. Ami sleeps in my room and goes to school with me. So far we fight only once a week, when *The Children's World* arrives; we fight about who's going to have the first chance to solve the puzzles. One Friday morning, when Nimrod came to visit Ricky and found two pupils in the classroom, he sighed and said, "Too bad—this is no longer the tiniest school in the State of Israel. The title is

181

now held by the Gilgal settlement in the Jordan Cleft. . . ."

I'm at the end of my story, at last. Everything is now behind us, and soon it will be impossible to tell what happened here between Yom Kippur and Simhat-Torah. The farm is the way it used to be, and the only sign of war is the blown-out piece in the big boulder. Only in summer can you see the scar on my arm.

Late in November, Ricky came with my new teacher, Yona from Nes-Tziyona. A plump, laughing girl. Ami is really in love with her, and she's cute. But I'll never forget Ricky.

The next day Yona talked about things that had happened to each of us during the past few months. Then she had us write a composition: "My Wartime Experiences." Ami wrote three and a half pages. I was going to write five or six pages, at most, and suddenly I found that I had written a whole book. Isn't that something?

Well, what can you do? Life's full of surprises. But I already wrote this too, way back in the first chapter.

Glossary

High Holidays - Rosh Hashana, the Jewish
New Year, and Yom Kippur,
the Day of Atonement, which
is the holiest day on the Jewish calendar. The High Holidays fall in early autumn.

Lehitraot - "Be seeing you" in Hebrew.

Mazal tov - "Good luck" in Hebrew.

Passover - Spring holiday commemorating the
deliverance of the Israelites from
slavery in Egypt 3500 years ago.

Sabbath - the Day of Rest (Saturday).

Seder - festive supper on Passover Eve.

Shalom/Salaam - Hebrew and Arabic words,
respectively, both meaning
"hello," "good-bye" and
"peace."

Simhat-Torah - last day of Succot festival,
"Rejoicing in the Law."

Succot - The Feast of Tabernacles, a thanks-
giving festival celebrated five days
after Yom Kippur.

Yom Kippur War - surprise attack by Egypt
on Israeli forces at the
Suez Canal, and by Syria

in the Golan Heights,
launched on Yom Kippur
1973.

Zahal - Israel defense forces (abbreviation of
Zva Haganah Le'yisrael).

About the Author

Uriel Ofek is one of Israel's foremost children's writers. He has published over thirty-five books for children and concerning children's literature, including Hebrew translations of world classics. In 1976 he won the Hans Christian Andersen Certificate of Honor of the International Board of Books for Young People, receiving international recognition. During his 1978 tour of the United States he gave the prestigious May Hill Arbuthnot lecture on children's literature.

A native-born Israeli, Dr. Ofek was captured during Israel's War of Independence in 1948 and, imprisoned in an Arab camp, "learned," he writes, "to understand the Arab soldiers and even to like many of them." He says of Smoke Over Golan, *"In spite of its title, it is not only a war story, but a book about peace and friendship."*

Dr. Ofek and his wife, writer Bina Ofek, live in Israel, as do their two daughters.